Wonderful Counselor

A Love Story

AMANDA ELYSE BLEAK, MS, LMHC
LICENSED MENTAL HEALTH COUNSELOR

Published by Mindstir Media, LLC
45 Lafayette Rd | Suite 181| North Hampton, NH 03862 | USA
1.800.767.0531 | www.mindstirmedia.com

Cover Photo Model: Olivia Elyse Bleak: oliviaelysebleak.com

Printed in the United States of America
ISBN-13: 978-1-958729-40-3

Dedication

For the Glory of God Alone

To all of those who loved me wrong
And sent me on a journey long,
Which brought me to true love that's right,
Embraced by God's never-ending
Mercy, Love, and Light!
Thank you ...

To the Reader

This is a work of intertwined, fictitious stories that come to life in one of the most beautiful and historic cities in the world, St. Augustine, Florida. The true message is the greatest non-fiction truth of all ~ Jesus, Son of the One and Only true God, loves you and died for you! All likeness to actual people and events is coincidental. No ethical lines have been crossed and no therapist-client confidentiality has been broken. The most important thing to know about me is that I am a Christ-follower who, at a young age, was taught a life of religion but hungered for relationship. Early childhood trauma tainted my understanding of human relationships and God's love for me. Trudging through many valleys and finally surrendering all that I am to my Creator has brought me healing and a passion to help others heal. I now offer pieces of my heart and the hearts I have met along the way, to you. I hope the transparency in this book catches hold of you. I hope you identify with a character, a journey, a struggle, a hope, or a truth, and are inspired to seek the only Source of Joy. Beware skeptics and theologians! Your scrutiny is expected, but not feared. If you dare read on, I challenge you to embrace this story with your hearts, not just your intellects—for I am just a seed planter...

Chapter 1

"You intended to harm me, but God intended it for good to accomplish what is now being done, the saving of many lives." Genesis 50:20

With an unsteady hand, Lillian Reynolds locked the door to her private practice counseling office located in a small, Spanish-style cottage in the backyard of her residence. The warm rain poured hard, making her keys slick and vision blurred.

"Perfect!" she muttered sarcastically. "God is drenching me with his disappointment from the get-go," she whispered to herself. It occurred to her that the weather was a sign to not do what she was getting ready to do or she might surely be struck by lightning. Shaking her head, she couldn't believe that her life seemed to have come full circle and she was only thirty-three. Struggling to hold her umbrella to protect her briefcase, the short walk to the car left her drenched and irritated. Its contents contained irreplaceable documentation that still needed to be uploaded on her computer. In the trunk sat her already-packed suitcase. She didn't plan to go back into her house after her last therapy session; she needed to get on the road.

Lillian had no reason to be in such a hurry, but nervous energy made her movements seem rushed and disjointed. She had no need to bring her briefcase, but it seemed to fit the façade. She'd concocted a bogus conference on trauma-focused play therapy to explain to her husband why she'd be away for the whole weekend. He wouldn't be rushing home anytime soon. The hotel she booked in Coral Gables would accept a check-in at any time. She practically knew everyone on staff. After all, Joshua and Lillian Reynolds were regulars. Four or five times a year, they'd book a stay to attend alumni events at the University of Miami or to visit some of their favorite places they'd frequented when dating. Catching the homecoming football game in the fall meant welcomed smells and sounds that brought back the energy and nostalgia of their early beginnings.

Lillian seldom made the trip alone though. She didn't enjoy herself as much when she went solo, even if it was for work. She missed Joshua. Miami was their city, the city where they fell in love, and neither one of them wanted to be there without the other. This Thursday evening, however, would be her first trip to South Florida without her husband, perpetuated by a lie, for a task she was reasonably certain would plague her conscience forever.

Lillian fleetingly glanced at her cell phone to make sure that it was still just past noon. *It all feels so strange*, she thought, rubbing her forehead. Normally, she booked clients through dinnertime on Thursdays, so she could have a lighter Friday. But she hadn't booked any afternoon sessions today in preparation for her trip. Joshua wouldn't be home from teaching until nearly 11 p.m., after his one weekly, late-night class and routine office duties. Her drive would take her about six hours with traffic. Conflicted about leaving or the trip itself, or both, she considered some liquid courage. *Why not?* she reasoned. *It had to be 5 o'clock SOMEWHERE, right?*

She certainly had time to go back inside, dry off, and get one drink to calm her nerves at her favorite local establishment. Ironically, the rain ended as soon as she made up her mind. As if it agreed with her, the rain seemed to patter, *Go ahead, Lil, you can even walk, and it's only one drink*, as it withdrew up into the full, retreating clouds.

Lillian navigated back across the slippery driveway in her high-heeled sandal wedges and reentered her home. She always felt confident in her "tall shoes" and "high heels." She often joked with Joshua that she wanted to enter a race running in heels and she bet she could win, if not come in a close second.

Lillian worked long hours and endless days to get to this point in her career. This is what she'd always wanted, a private mental health practice in a detached cottage on her own property. It consisted of a historic two-story home in St. Augustine, her favorite city in the world. Of course, it had a separate private entrance and a privacy hedgerow along a tall privacy fence separating her personal life from her professional life while merging the two on the same property.

She pushed her way through the orange-tiled foyer, tripping on a dog toy. Knocking over her potted Lady Palm, she was robustly greeted with licks and wags by her loyal, favorite friend Leo, the family three-year-old dachshund. He was blessed with beautiful, long, strawberry-blonde hair. It was an enviable shade many women spent hours and dollars trying to obtain at salons. Leo was short for Leonidas, the legendary King of Sparta—Joshua's idea. Her husband loved everything about ancient world history, specifically anything to do with the Greeks. He was a popular young professor at Flagler College known for his passion for antiquities, enthusiasm for religion, and his commitment to connecting with his students.

"Hey buddy, my little pumpkin-spiced latte with extra whip! Mommy's back already!" Lillian called as she dropped to her knees to scratch his ears and welcome his sloppy kisses. The whipped cream nickname came from the patches of white on Leo's neck and chest. Rubbing his soft belly, she felt bad for getting his hopes up. He was the other reason she already had her car packed and had not planned to reenter her house. She didn't want to say good-bye again and hear his cries of disappointment.

Looking down at his adorable face, his eyes seemed elated to have her company again. He had pouted when she packed her suitcase earlier that morning. He seemed to know that this was Joshua's one late night, and it was as if he sensed with the packing that he would be alone longer than usual...or was she just projecting?

He had curled up on the bed, placed his head on his paws, and watched her intentionally place each item in each specific bag—the shirt as it disappeared in the suitcase, the blush tucked away in the makeup case. Item by item, his eyes followed, like a tennis match, back and forth. He used his best distraction tactic and rolled over on his back. Exposing his belly and the patches of white fur, he had waited to be caressed, submitting then too.

The separations were always hard on Lillian. She would reassure him and promised to bring him a special treat from each destination. She couldn't help but laugh out loud when she flew to Dallas for a conference on child abuse the previous year and found one of his favorite toys, a purple octopus, inside her suitcase. He must have placed it there when she was busy running around the bedroom throwing clothes in, not paying much attention. She thought it was his way of saying, *"Don't forget about me, Mom."* Now, she always double-checked her bags, just to make sure he didn't climb in himself.

Still rubbing Leo's belly, her conflicted emotions resurfaced. A necessary trip. A necessary lie. A necessary sacrifice, to set things straight…right?

Chapter 2

C oming up with a plausible lie had been the easy part once the deci-sion had been made. Her profession held her to earning continuing education units, or CEUs. Constant emails and newsletters showed up advertising classes. She had to meet a deadline every two years to keep her mental health license current. Traditionally, she'd obtain the CEUs locally or online, never wanting to leave her husband or Leo for more than a few hours. Sometimes, the topic of the training was just too good to miss, requiring her to travel, like the one in Dallas when Leo had sent his toy along. This time, she'd purposefully sought out a fake conference in Coral Gables, to cover her real plans and do what was destined. She had bar-gained with herself and even justified it to Joshua by insisting that the peri-odic, "face-to-face interaction" with other professionals was the key to not losing the human touch. She reasoned that so many people complacently texted and social media'd their way through life and missed out on facial expressions and having the chance to peer into another's soul. Being physi-cally present was so important. Or at least that had been her excuse.

She lobbied that Coral Gables was offering the specific topic she was interested in to enhance her "trauma" niche—children who survived human trafficking. It was not exactly a lie. She had completed the compre-hensive training online just the previous week and gained the knowledge she would need if he asked how the training was.

Wow, Lil, she thought. *How premeditated and sociopathic of you*, her inner dialogue condemned her.

To Lillian, Joshua seemed to have noticed a change in her over the past several weeks, or maybe it was a month, she thought. But instead of pushing, he'd offer a sweet kiss, and a prayer for safe travels while holding her forearms a little tighter and longer than usual. It made her deception weigh even heavier on her heart as she backed up and turned away.

"You know how much I love you and that you can talk to me about anything, right?" His last words echoed in her ears. His gaze seemed to penetrate right into her guilty soul.

"I love you too, Joshua," she replied, avoiding altogether the opportunity he'd deliberately opened.

Remembering her mission to grab a quick drink, Lillian changed quickly out of her wet clothes, continuing to use her own self-talk tools to remind herself to slow down. She had struggled with anxiety since she was three years old. She could still remember the butterflies in her stomach throughout her preschool experience at Jack and Jill Nursery School.

"The butterflies are back in my tummy," she would raise her hand and tell her teacher. Her gentle, maternal teacher would kneel at her eye level and coach her to take long, deep breaths to "blow them out and set them free." She had since lost count of how many children, adolescents, and adults she too had taught relaxation breathing to since becoming a therapist. *Makes sense*, she thought during graduate school, *my childhood experiences were the proving ground that forged the therapist I am today.*

But then her father's unwanted voice echoed in her mind, "Choose to wear the crown of beauty, Lil; let God wipe away your ashes." Her father, a Protestant pastor at a Lutheran Church, always threw nuggets of scripture at Lillian instead of providing the quality time she knew now as a therapist that she had so desperately needed. As if as a child and young teenager, she was supposed to relate to the "year of the Lord's favor" described in the Old Testament by the prophet Isaiah.

"Really, Dad? Crowns and ashes?" She remembered her confusion, frustration, and annoyance at his hollow words. Then the predictable twinge of guilt followed like a frequent, unwelcome friend. Today was even worse—guilt compounding guilt, and frustration surfacing, she shook free of the memory and grabbed Leo's leash.

"Come on, boy, let's go get us a drink."

Chapter 3

With purpose, Lillian headed east on Valencia Street and turned north on Sevilla Street, toward the Memorial Presbyterian Church looming majestically at the corner, claiming a large space with authority. It was a beautiful church, modeled after St. Marks in Venice, Italy. The solid structure with stained glass held the entombed bodies of Henry Flagler and several family members. Henry Flagler was a railroad and hotel baron who put St. Augustine on the map for winter destinations back in the late 1800s. Rich northern snowbirds booked one of three grand southern hotels to escape the harsh winters. The crown jewel was the Ponce de Leon, which now stood as Flagler College.

Lillian took a quick detour, leading Leo through the church's wrought iron gate into the Memorial Garden that circled behind the property—their own secret passageway. Encompassed by shadows and overflowing with tranquility, she reflected on the first time she had brought Joshua there. It was a warm afternoon walk after they had moved into their new home and unpacked several boxes. She'd instructed him to close his eyes and trust her to safely lead him to one of her favorite spots she had discovered in the city. Joshua, so hopelessly in love with Lillian that he would have let her lead him down a dark and ominous road with glowing warning signs stating, *turn back now or die a long slow death*, just took her hand. That was Joshua, Lillian thought. He was always the solid, immovable rock, ever present, standing firm in treacherous storms at all costs. His nobleness bullied her sometimes by stirring up her insecurities and challenging her that she'd never be worthy of him.

But on that day, back in the garden together, they had been equals. She had positioned herself behind him, with his strong back pressing against her breasts, savoring a flash of pleasure that shot through her core.

"Take a deep breath!" she commanded. She wrapped her hands around his face and covered his eyes, whispering, "One, two, three, now open!" She directed his head up towards the domed roof while keeping her hands at the sides of his head like horse blinders.

"See, my love, if you stand right here and block out the world, it's as if you really are in Italy!" she whispered again. Joshua wove his fingers through Lillian's without words. As if Lillian could feel the shift in Joshua's chest, she unwrapped her fingers from his and cupped them over his heart. For several years, they had talked about going to Italy together and he'd promised to take her but hadn't yet.

"Baby, it's okay, this is good enough for now. This can be my Rome and you are my king." The kiss that followed was tender and deep, almost desperate. Actually, it was the kiss that so many kisses afterwards would be compared to and it would be used as a frame of reference for her. Thinking back, Lillian realized it was a kiss that had become harder to recreate these past few weeks. Lillian impatiently pushed away the memory and gently reprimanded Leo for lifting his leg on the sanctified ground.

As she and her long-haired escort passed through the inner courtyard of the church, beyond the area where they had pretended it was Rome, a negative feeling engulfed her. It happened every time. Dragging her fingertips gently across the cold, unwelcoming feel of the rough coquina wall near the side of the building, Lillian couldn't help but acknowledge it seemed symbolic. The negative feelings church offered her growing up grated roughly across her young heart in much the same way the wall felt against her skin. After all, she was the daughter of a pastor. She should be on fire for God. She should get it more than anybody, right?

She often beat herself up about it. She might as well have been Catholic, wearing her Catholic guilt like a badge of honor. However, Lutherans were close enough; they were Catholic-lite. She avoided the conversation with her father, a man with tireless time and energy for saving others' souls, but rarely noticed the ones inside his own home. Insecurities and imperfections weren't welcomed or really even addressed in their house. So, she learned how to wear a mask and pretend to be someone she was not, at an early age. She learned how to portray what her dad, and eventually the world, thought she should be on the outside and wrestle with who she really was on the inside.

Chapter 4

Not quite ready to move forward out of the church garden, she hesitated and once again reached out to brush her fingers against the limestone mixed with broken shells. Memories of a forbidden love affair flooded in. The texture against her hand felt rough, like his short facial hair against her neck and cheek. She had been barely eighteen, and the summer had been a hot, muggy one. She was living in South Florida—in Coral Gables, to be exact—and attending her last youth event before beginning college at the University of Miami. The function was just a few miles from her home and father's church and was her last chance for some closure with friends and mentors from her high-school days.

Her youth pastor had told her she was the most beautiful being he had ever seen. *A gift from God*. Those epic words were ones she never heard from her father and maybe heard from her mother once, if at all, but certainly not those exact words. Or maybe her mother had never really spoken them, and it was her desperate hoping that had her imagining that she had once said them—just once. The trained therapist in Lillian could look back and realize those words had skillfully set the trap. They were the catalyst for the perfect storm. Lillian had already spent many days and nights trusting her youth pastor, building an innocent four-year relationship, throughout her entire high-school career.

He had watched her grow and blossom into a woman while offering her what she had thought was biblical theology. In return, she had led his three daughters around at Vacation Bible School every summer, teaching songs and doing activities that promoted a tangible God. His family provided the compassion and attention that Lillian rarely experienced in her own home. Now she recognized just how vulnerable and trusting she had been. Especially after her painful high-school relationship breakup that was a focus of processing and confiding in him throughout the summer before college. That's not to say that Lillian felt the youth pastor had been intentionally corrupt or evil. He had modeled goodness and godliness until… He had slowly allowed himself to become wrapped up in his own selfish needs and it wasn't long before he began to twist his theology to fit his fleshly desires. He had justified fondling and caressing her by calling it love, the greatest commandment of all. He had justified the abortion too; when Lillian found out she was five weeks pregnant the fall of her freshman year of college, the solution had been his suggestion. Remembering the terrifying first symptoms of sore breasts and morning sickness just five weeks after the night of conception, Lillian had condemned herself that the discomfort was payback for the dishonesty that had produced the fetus. Now, she realized it was actually a child planted in her womb in a tangle of deceit not of her own making. Then there was the awful way the youth pastor had manipulated his version of theology to pressure her to end the pregnancy.

"It's not murder, Lil," he had urged. "It's making a situation go away that could cause many people a lot of pain. It's the right thing to do. Think of the embarrassment for your father—for the church! You would be an outcast if people found out that you pursued me, that you caused all this by tempting me with your sweet beauty," he explained. Lillian recalled how confused she had been. *YOU pursued ME; you caused all this*, she had thought. Those seven simple words, spoken that stifling, hot day, would remain imprinted in her brain indefinitely; it set her up for continual, automatic, negative thoughts that she battled to recognize and replace for many years. Her translation had been: *It's all my fault. I'm a whore.* He had driven her to the clinic on a Friday morning and handed her five hundred dollars cash. Callously dropping her in the parking lot and driving off, he reinforced the sense of isolation and self-doubt she now knew would become a hallmark of her young adult life. She skipped three classes, walking back to her dorm slowly and nauseously after it was over. She had faked the stomach flu that weekend in a desperate bid for solitude. To avoid the virus, her roommate agreeably stayed in her boyfriend's dorm. The cramps had been unbearable, and the blood clots came in unrelenting waves, she remembered. She had thought for sure she would bleed out, organs and all, until there was nothing left or until she was an empty shell covered in bone and skin, lifeless, her soul destined to burn in hell. She was a murderer, or at least that is how she was sure some would see her, especially those in the house of God. Her baby's father, the youth pastor, had been a different story altogether though. He changed the truth to fit his narrative. So relieved to be off the hook, he now barely acknowledged her. But the worst had been the nightmares that followed. Lillian began imagining a daughter, with tiny quivering lips and barely identifiable fingernails being insensitively and aggressively vacuumed from her uterus, not even given a chance to try life. It didn't matter that her child was still substantially unformed yet. The dreams of torment had just kept coming. By Monday morning, she was back in class, a paler, thinner, haunted version of herself.

The change in her demeanor did not go unnoticed to the trained eye. "Are you feeling alright, Lil?" her philosophy professor had asked, pulling her aside after class. Dr. Suarez had a warm smile, salt and pepper hair that suggested wisdom, and mocha skin that always reminded her of the perfect summer tan.

"Oh sure, I'm just getting over the twenty-four-hour flu, Dr. Suarez, no worries," Lillian had weakly lied and shuffled for the door. He furrowed his brow at her for a second, then told her to drink electrolytes, and stay away from the wild parties and alcohol her peers would be offering over the weekend.

"You have too much potential for that foolishness. You can do great things, Ms. Lillian," he urged. Lillian had frozen for a second, then she had forced a smile and nodded. As she walked away, she thought, *I wish that was the only trouble I had to worry about falling into.*

Predictably, her youth pastor had lost interest in her after the procedure. Unless she had just been imagining it, he seemed to place his arm around his wife a little bit tighter in the pew on the following Sunday mornings. He avoided eye contact. She may as well have been invisible to him. Lillian had stopped attending church, ready to lie to her father that she wanted to make new connections at an on-campus church; but her explanation turned out to be unnecessary, because he didn't seem to notice and never asked. Lillian never confronted or saw the youth pastor again in person after leaving the church, but a day never passed that she did not visit him in her mind, flogging herself mentally for her failure.

Chapter 5

Now, adult, professional, but still self-punishing, Lillian continued her St. Augustine walk north on Sevilla Street. It brought her to the Ancient City Baptist Church and then, looking east down Carrera Street, she quickly spotted the Methodist Church on the corner. She stopped briefly in response to Leo's preoccupation with a tree, and her mind wandered for a moment.

"There should be a large sign out front of the Baptist church reading, 'We immerse you here,' and 'Sprinkling is okay by us' outside of the Methodist Church," she told Leo. Since her father's people were Lutheran, they sprinkled. Lillian remembered the baptizing debates between her father and his fellow clergy from different denominations. Lillian still questioned why the beautiful sacrament of baptism and that public acknowledgment of obedience to one's faith was so different among the many denominations of Christ followers.

Was it really God's intent for it to be so divided and complicated? Did mankind really need different rules among the different denominations? Didn't it just distract from the overall message? Then there was the Catholic church, not on the same two city blocks as these other three churches. No, it had its own place in town, standing alone on its own street, set apart. It was a church riddled with its own traditions and liturgical practices, its rituals seemed to focus predominantly on rules and less on a personal relationship with Jesus. They had the stipulation that parishioners had to confess their sins to a priest, though the Bible taught Jesus' crucifixion put an end to that need. The "veil" was torn, and all have direct access to God. However, the contradiction and Christ's sacrifice and the need for a priest still goes unaddressed today. How many clients did Lillian counsel who were more confused about their spirituality and felt less connected to God even after years of church attendance?

Turning South on Cordova Street, Lillian approached her favorite corner bar, and her lips parted in a smile. Purposely shoving those frustrating, conflicting memories into one of her handy mental compartments, she slammed the metaphorical door on her thought-debate. The sign hanging off the porch paid homage to *Gone with the Wind*, an epic Civil War drama and beautiful, tragic love story. Scarlett O'Hara's offered live music and an instant shot of adrenaline every time she stepped on the property, and the outdoor seating allowed Leo to be her plus-one. Instinctively, she tucked herself into a table near the corner of the porch and made eye contact with the waiter. He brought Leo a bowl of water on the rocks and a sweet red wine for her; never a need to ask—it was Lillian's usual. It was always delicious. She was convinced it had to be similar in taste to the wine that Jesus had created from jars of water at the wedding feast in Cana, where he performed his first miracle. The vintage was fun to say: "Sangua Di Guida," an Italian wine, translated, "The Blood of Judas." Legend offered a few explanations for the name. Lillian's favorite was the one that explained that the monks who made the wine in Lombardy, Italy, decided to give it a terrifying name to discourage nuns who would break in and overindulge in the sweet nectar. The name didn't work, however. The nuns could not resist the sweet, bubbly drink and continued to enjoy it.

"To the nuns! To the monks!" Lillian smiled and lifted her glass to Leo.

Chapter 6

Leo's loud, sloppy slurps attracted attention from couples and college co-eds sitting nearby. But Lillian was almost immune to the giggles and glances. Usually, it only took one gulp of wine for her to feel the relaxation rush through her body. It reminded her of the addiction stories she'd listened to during her rigorous graduate-school internship. She counseled men and women suffering from substance abuse, in group settings, and then individually with pregnant or new mothers who needed methadone for opioid- and drug-withdrawal symptoms and cravings. She understood the minds of people struggling with an addiction, a quick-fix substance they were using to escape their life struggles. She also knew that when the substance wore off, the issue was still there, still staring you down. The difference was that things actually seemed worse because you were sober. And the sober you was well aware that you'd be labeled an addict—drugs, alcohol, pornography, gambling, it didn't matter which. The world would be sure to judge you.

"Mental health and addictions—welcome to the frontlines! You will either thrive here or perish. Of course, we can smell the perishable interns a mile away, and we don't waste time bringing them on board. So welcome, newbie!" She would never forget those first words, spoken by her supervisor on her first day at The Grotto, a tucked-away retreat where clients could heal, redefine, and rediscover life's treasures. She truly valued her internship during graduate school, working with the combination of addictions and mental health.

Lillian had wrestled with the backhanded compliment from her boss, trying to convince herself that it was praise, trying to believe that maybe her clinical supervisor saw something in her that she was unable and unwilling to see or believe about herself. She was more like a duck than an eagle or even a swan. While she mostly appeared cool and calm on the surface, her legs were paddling fast as hell under the water to keep herself afloat. Her childhood anxiety was never too far from the surface and increased the first week she began the internship. However, it slowly diminished over time. The more she connected with her clients and the more stories she heard, the more she found her groove. She realized that she was not so different from them. They chose substances to avoid their issues, while Lillian chose deception, a kind of mask-wearing, to avoid hers.

Her clients loved her. Her own flaws made her disarmingly non-judgmental and approachable with most of them. There were always a few with thick, tall walls to break through that required extra time and patience. Grad school had drilled into her the importance of balancing "unconditional positive regard" with "compassionate confrontation" as the keys to effective treatment. Veteran therapists often needed a sabbatical to regain positivity and neutrality. They had the dangerous potential of growing cynical and hopeless from years of watching their clients relapse and cycle back through the system. It took consistent self-care plans, which included therapists seeking their own therapy, to maintain compassion and the healthy balance of separating work from life. Lillian was remarkably good at maintaining that balance.

Finishing her internship with the study of the challenge of addictions, she chose her first paying job post-graduation at a non-profit mental health agency. She had specialized in children, adolescents, and families with an array of mental health diagnoses. She hadn't made that choice to run from the addiction-plagued clients—they still popped up from time to time. However, she gained confidence in her ability to help people. She had noticed three patterns in her adult addiction clients: self-medicating mental illness symptoms, unresolved childhood trauma, or "the doctor gave me painkillers; I liked the high and I couldn't stop" issue. Interestingly, many clients in group sessions reported they remembered their first high from the dentist's chair. While it was no big deal to many patients, some people's brain chemistry demanded more.

She had thought that by working with children, she could teach them healthy coping skills early, point out their strengths, and steer them away from the temptation to experiment with drugs. She had thought that the earlier she could get to them, the healthier the next generation would be, avoiding the addiction route all together. At least that was how she had envisioned it in her little corner of the world.

Lillian had immediately gotten twenty-five clients on her caseload as an outpatient therapist. That doubled within the first year. Fifty clients created unimaginable paperwork demands and court testimony expectations. She became close with a colleague, an art therapist, who shared several innovative art therapy techniques. Together, they facilitated art therapy groups for several years, giving her priceless creative techniques to incorporate in therapy sessions when talk therapy was not enough to get a client from point A to point B.

Lillian served her families diligently and passionately for seven long years at the non-profit agency. In return, she grew comfortable and competent to work with most issues and diagnoses. She worked side-by-side with child psychiatrists who prescribed psychotropic medications to offer their clients' brains the needed chemical mixture to alleviate symptoms. The meds provided relief when therapy alone had not shown progress toward achieving treatment plan goals.

Like lots of other therapists, low pay and graduate student loan obligations drove her to secure side work in the evenings and on the weekends, seeing clients for the Child Protection Team. In that environment, she had realized a passion for working with sexual abuse survivors and their non-offending caregivers. It illustrated to Lillian the insidious work of the dark side and the need for the light of God. Although she struggled with embracing the light of God fully within herself, ironically, she was able to easily offer it to others. She quickly had gained confidence as an advocate for children, was recognized officially as an expert court testimony witness, and honed her evidence-based trauma techniques with precision and dedication.

Now, remembering her first day in court as an expert witness for a termination of parental rights hearing, she cringes. She had wanted an invisibility cloak that day. It was that bad.

"Mrs. Reynolds, how long have you been specializing in abuse cases?" the defendant's lawyer asked.

"Twelve weeks," she nervously responded.

"And do you consider yourself an expert?" he followed up.

"No. I do not," she maintained again, nervously. The attorney laughed and the judge smiled. The victim's attorney followed up by combing through Lillian's resume' and verbally listed her credentials, including her extensive trauma background and certifications. The court contended that she was indeed their expert witness, whether she felt like it or not, and she continued with her testimony. From that day forward, she determined to know her worth regarding her profession, despite her conflicting personal feelings. Feelings could not always be trusted. She had adopted a "fake it until you make it" mantra that gave her confidence when she walked through the courtroom doors each day. Every time, she repeated it faithfully until, one day, she no longer had to fake it. She had realized out of the blue that she was confident in her knowledge and experiences. She had heard herself share facts, listen closely, and answer slowly. She had learned the lawyers' tactics and was not shy to say "I don't know; I don't have a crystal ball" when they tried their hardest to get her to say something that would benefit their case but was beyond her scope of practice or inappropriate for her to answer. She had realized she knew trauma and she knew how to advocate for her clients. She also knew how to use taking a drink from a water bottle to stop and think and maintain control when an opposing attorney was using their best theatrics. She had realized that she had finally made it. There was no faking it anymore.

Chapter 7

Sitting in Scarlett O'Hara's, still twirling the stem of the wineglass between her fingers, Lillian waved away a second glass of wine already being delivered by the waiter.

"Hey, Lil! It's our lunch happy hour, remember? Two for one!" exclaimed Brent, the charismatic waiter, working his way through college on generous tips provided by tipsy consumers who were mesmerized by his green eyes and irresistible smile. No doubt he bleached those spectacularly white teeth, Lillian had suspected for months. He was already placing the second glass on the table in front of her. Winking at the bartender, he confirmed that the two of them were partners in crime, smoothly tempting customers into "just one more drink," which turned into several more drinks. Clever to gently keep lowering inhibitions and subsequently increasing the anticipated tips.

Lillian noticed two male co-eds sitting adjacent to her, seemingly not trying hard to hide their admiration of her long, tan, muscular legs, forged by long early-morning runs. Lillian smiled as she entertained the possibility that her years of academic hard work and the battles with her personal demons had not diminished some of her outward beauty. Then, one of the guys half-whispered, "Hey, good boy!" and she quickly realized their attention was actually on Leo, who was fast asleep and leaning against her foot with his head placed upon his paws. Her slight flush of satisfaction disappeared, leaving her a little deflated. Just a second behind that thought was a reminder of the dark secret she carried inside of her. Wow, she had loitered enough, her conscience scolded her. Sliding the stemmed glass toward the center of the table, she knew she needed to move along so she could get to Coral Gables before midnight. She paid her bill and of course over-tipped her waiter for both glasses. Two identical, crimson glasses of wine remained untouched on the table as she walked away.

She left the comfort of the corner bar, heading south on Cordova until she connected to Valencia again and turned west towards home. Lillian was comforted by the tradition of following her typical walking pattern to and from Scarlett O'Hara's. She essentially completed a rectangle pattern that took her by an art gallery, a used bookstore, and a clothing boutique that Leo stopped at instinctively, waiting for the free treat offered by the store owner. Walking adjacent to Flagler College always brought back memories of clients and reminded her of the essential connection between her academic studies and the real-life practice of those concepts. Today, it was Hannah who came to mind. Hannah was one of the first clients she saw when she had started her private practice just two years prior.

Chapter 8

According to Hannah, her life reeked of mediocrity. She was average height for a nineteen-year-old girl; she was also average intelligence and looks, at least by her own standards.

"And to add to all of that," she proclaimed in her first session with Lillian, presenting with mild anxiety and what appeared to be an existential crisis, "My name is the exact same spelled frontwards as backwards!" Lillian felt a smile break open inside herself as she sensed a uniquely beautiful soul before her. She suspected that it would take several sessions to get Hannah to consider acknowledging that truth.

"Well, so your name is a palindrome! That's unique, Hannah. Not many people can say that, not ordinary at all." Lillian intentionally validated Hannah's frustration by reflecting and acknowledging exactly what she said, then added a little humor to keep it light, friendly, and therapeutically build "rapport."

As their sessions increased, Lillian learned that Hannah had the gift of storytelling. There were rarely quiet moments to sit in silent stillness and reflect in her sessions. She had started by explaining that she lived in a mundane neighborhood filled with unexciting people, working routine jobs, and driving ordinary cars to get themselves through tedious days. Everything about her life was commonplace, she maintained. Nothing thrilling ever happened to Hannah or anyone in her family. Hannah always compared her life to her old neighbor Hope's. She called Hope the lucky girl who used to live down the street. Her great Aunt Lucille died and left Hope's family a sizable life insurance settlement. They put their house up for sale and moved into the gated community on the other side of town. That community boasted swimming pools in every backyard, and screened patios to keep out the annoyances of bugs, falling leaves, and voyeuristic neighbors. There was a fancy key-code pad at the gated entrance to the neighborhood that required a secret six-digit number to cross through the barrier into the inaccessible world. Hannah liked to imagine frustrated residents forgetting their codes, unable to get in. Or the key-code pads breaking down, people trapped, or doomed to sit outside the eight-foot wall indefinitely.

"Serves them right," she proclaimed, laughing out loud, "trying to strip the mediocre from their remote community."

"Do you think it is better to be a prisoner inside the perfectly landscaped utopia or locked outside, where you don't have any of your belongings, but you have access to the rest of humanity?" Lillian had inquired.

"Much better to be on the outside, free to fly, not caged in, for sure," Hannah affirmed.

Throughout the sessions, Hannah had continued to share about another friend, Rose, who had a rich uncle who lived in a three-story log cabin on a lake in Georgia. With every visit they made to the cabin, Rose's four brothers quickly claimed the third floor as their own secluded hideaway. It was incredibly designed with wall-to-wall windows overlooking their small, saltless ocean, surrounded by tall, thick pine trees. They were like fish-in-a-bowl, spied upon by the birds of the sky who found shelter in the branches of the infinite foliage. The birds dutifully protected the secrets of all that went on up there: the wrestling matches, pool tournaments, the sweet treats snuck up after all the adults were preoccupied with card games and reminiscing. As the kids played, the adults sipped on "drink drinks," their made-up term for alcoholic adult beverages. Monitoring of the children upstairs faded with the stories of old so that even the occasional bang from the top floor went unnoticed through the laughter and connecting.

"The smell of clean air really grabs hold of you there," Hannah had explained, after she returned from a week's visit, still shocked her mother had let her escape with Rose.

Hannah had described how it seemed that your thoughts were clearer and any despair that you may have brought with you was scattered as soon as you stepped out on the extraordinary ground. A feeling of peace seemed to hang over the lake population, a peace that Hannah acknowledged she longed to know in her own world. Rose's family typically spent long weekends and summers at the cabin, jet skiing and fishing, talking into the darkness of the night, all nestled around bonfires. The glow of the fires, all the while, held on to the stories told, long after the storytellers fell into deep, restful slumber. The Georgia cabin was a place where time stood still, real-world bills never had to be paid, and the endless fish fries and barbeques made restaurants unnecessary.

Chapter 9

Hannah's graphic recollections had often propelled Lillian back to her own childhood lake house visits every summer. While her family had lived in Royal Oak, Michigan, her mom's parents had owned a picturesque, lake-front property which included a house, cottage, and sauna in Michigan's Upper Peninsula, across the Mackinaw Bridge on Lake Superior. From elementary through middle school, Lillian had anticipated the summers on Lake Superior. Sadly, that was before her father had accepted a head pastor position with a larger congregation in South Florida, just a month before she had started high school.

At the time, her father had justified the drastic move across the country as a fresh start that would do them good after the "accident." Now, Lillian recognized the destructive mischaracterization of the term "accident" used to describe what had actually happened. The "accident" he insisted on calling the event was one from which Lillian still had not fully healed. Her training had taught her that healing could only come from facing the truth; perpetuating a lie to feel better just delayed healing.

Her maternal grandparents had lived off a dirt road on Lake Superior, in an area called Keweenaw Bay, along with several other generations of immigrated Finlanders. They all had equipped their properties with personal saunas—a key reflection of their cultural heritage. Lillian enjoyed this unique aspect of her ancestry. Ironically, she had also inadvertently learned important human anatomy in those saunas. Whether it was because a towel unexpectedly slipped off a relative or the casual, flapping shower curtains offered minimal true privacy, she quickly had learned the difference between men and women.

She had learned to love to sweat because of how freeing it felt to allow a cleansing of toxins through her pores. She always associated a sense of safety and well-being with the sanctity of the sauna, and it had always been exciting when her mummo, grandmother in Finnish, would give her permission to pour more water on the rocks. The steam that hissed forward was thick and penetrating, making breathing more difficult. But having to struggle some to breathe had made her feel alive. The mixture of smells of human sweat, wood, and fire became invigorating.

In the early days of each summer, she'd begun on the lower bench of the three-bench structured sauna, acclimating to the tiny, hot enclosure. In the small, dark room, the only light that had been offered came from a dim lightbulb on a pull-string and a small window, covered with a curtain that the occupant could choose to close or leave open. She remembered challenging herself to slowly move up to the second bench, and then finally the third, where the air was thickest. Some days, Lillian would put on her bathing suit and play sauna games with her lakeside friends. There was a local family with four children, two brothers and two sisters, who lived year-round, down the street. They had welcomed her visits and stories brought from south of the Mackinaw Bridge. Always stopping at the bridge to use the bathroom on her way to her grandparents, she'd gather snacks before crossing; she was their saltwater taffy supplier. She routinely greeted them with a three-pound bag that had shrunk to a two-pound bag by the time they arrived at her grandparents' property. It was the closest thing Lillian had known to having siblings.

As an only child, Lillian had relied on the companionship of her dog, Benji, a long-haired black and tan dachshund who had always been in step with her and ready for any outdoor adventures. He had been a constant comfort, burrowing under the covers, cuddling for hours, and offering protection with a deep, defending bark; she was sure if a black bear came out of the woods, Benji would defend her life and stand up to it as if it were only a squirrel. Whenever she had entered the sauna, he patiently laid outside the door, keeping guard while waiting for her exit.

The neighboring sibling group of four, Dean, Shelly, Braden, and Kelsey, waited yearly for her return through three long seasons. Their summer adventures included exploring the woods, canoeing up and down the coastline, hide-and-seek, and four-wheeling. However, the activity that had trumped all was their made-up sauna game. They would gather snuggly in the little, humid closet with their bathing suits on for as long as they could endure it, and then ran out, down the smooth man-made rock path, to enter the freezing cold lake. Then, when they could not bear the cold any longer, they'd run back up to the sauna and start the game all over again. Lillian had helped her grandfather lay the rock path out perfectly one summer, resulting in a beautiful, creative walkway that was a welcomed relief from the previous option of walking through itchy grass and dirt.

Lake Superior, the coldest lake of the Great Lakes, had faithfully awaited their hot bodies every summer, every trip down that walkway. One by one, they'd slowly climb off the dock into the shocking ice water. There was never any jumping or diving; it was too shallow and dangerous. The surface of the lake was often pristine and calm. It was like looking through glass. The bottom offered a treacherous combination of smooth and jagged rock. Lillian never made it through a summer without a scrape or bruise from the rocky shore and those slippery moss-covered rocks that demanded the footwear she refused to wear. The bottom of her left foot held her most prized scar, bearing a deep cut that had required eleven stitches.

Strangely, it was still a positive core memory for Lillian despite the considerable physical pain it had produced. It created an opportunity for her to live out her first romantic rescue fantasy, and the subject of that fantasy was the handsome older neighbor, Jeremiah. Etched deeply in her memories, the summer before her eighth-grade year, that rescue had found her nestled closely to Jeremiah in the back seat of her grandfather's truck, while he applied pressure to stop the bleeding cut. Using the closest thing he had available, Lillian remembered staring as he removed his checkered, collared, button-down and pressed the balled-up fabric against her foot. Her wide, pained eyes darted back and forth between the shirt and his tank top-strapped chest. She was thirteen and something inside her had awakened that year that left her feeling flushed and nervous around boys. As she recalled, it had been a tsunami of awakenings that summer.

"Mom! I'm bleeding from between my legs!" she couldn't forget yelling to her mom as she sat on the toilet, examining the murder scene.

"Oh Lillian, now? Did you bring anything?" Eventually her mother came to the door.

"No," Lillian replied, ashamed and deflated. Now, as a grown woman who found her voice, she wishes she would have said, "Since this has literally never happened before, I can't imagine why I would 'bring anything.' Isn't that your job as the mother?" She should have been sarcastic and condemning. Then, she should have followed up with, "Self-absorbed, sad excuse of a mother!" Instead, she wadded up toilet paper and ran to see Shelly at the other end of the road.

Shelly, at age 17, older and wiser, congratulated her and showed her how to put in a tampon by inserting one in herself. Lillian was shocked as she watched mesmerized and horrified. She had never seen another vagina that close. Shelly gave her a box of her own tampons from a stash under her bathroom sink.

"Ideally, you should use a pad until you're ready to have something inside you. Have you ever had something inside you?" Shelly asked with concern. Lillian, wide-eyed, shook her head no. Her heartbeat increased.

"I can't, I'm not ready!" Lillian affirmed. The thought of an object going into uncharted territory scared her.

"Are you sure? It's going to be hard to run around in the woods and impossible to jump in the lake with bulging toilet paper in your crotch," Shelly rationalized.

"Yeah, that's true," Lillian realized and stuffed her fears. "Okay, I can do it. Help me?" Lillian took a deep breath to prepare herself.

"You can make a baby now, so be careful when you're with a boy!" Shelly warned Lillian as she inserted the applicator and entered Lillian's sacred place. Lillian nodded and winced as the tampon pushed through tight tissue, a moment she imagined would be much different. Ceremonial, perhaps, including a bath with candles, her mother imparting wisdom about her future husband and motherhood while washing her hair and offering her a pre-bought box of maxi-pads, anticipating her daughter's rite of passage to womanhood. They would eat ice cream together and watch a movie that triggered emotions that they could relate to and talk about, making Lillian feel normal. Making Lillian feel important.

Chapter 10

Lillian's memories of her Lake Michigan summers would be incomplete and dull without including Jeremiah. He had been the good that came with the bad. Jeremiah lived next door in the summer months on his widower grandfather's property, as he helped maintain the house and garden, and had run errands. In exchange, his grandfather paid his college tuition at the technological college of engineering in the city of Houghton, north of their tucked-away community. Looking back, Lillian recognized that Jeremiah had the heart of a servant. She was sure he would have helped his grandfather without the tuition gift. She was also sure that his grandfather would have paid the tuition without Jeremiah's help. Their hearts were unified. Family counted above all; give without expecting anything in return was practiced and sharing what you had always happened.

After she had cut her foot open on the rocks, Jeremiah had stopped the blood flow while her grandfather drove south to the nearest emergency room. It was miles away, around winding roads, through the town of Baraga and into the village of L'Anse. The drive, which was normally long and tortuous for an impatient child, hadn't been long enough that time. Jeremiah's embrace had been gentle and protective. It had awakened in her a desire to be rescued by older men, and it felt euphoric. Now, Lillian recognized that the need had continued to manifest itself throughout her young life, with or without her permission. She wondered how differently her life's path would have been had her earthly father filled the role of protector that God intends for all fathers, instead of him focusing so fervently on helping others. As she had relaxed in his protective embrace, Jeremiah had gone on and on about being safe in the water and minding the jagged rocks.

"You should probably wear some type of protective footwear, Lil," he had insisted. She begged for him to come back to the examination room as her grandfather completed the paperwork. Clinging hard to his hand when the doctor had given her two shots, then a third in the wound to numb the location in preparation for stitches, she wept. Jeremiah had wiped her tears gently while doing his best to distract her with a game of twenty questions.

The ride back home had included a stop for food. Her grandfather's philosophy was that an empty bowel and full stomach could make almost everything better. Burgers and root beer floats in the back of the truck bed were a perfect picnic. If only her grandfather would go away, Lillian had thought, so she could have considered this their first date. Jeremiah hoisted her up onto a blanket that he had carefully folded and placed there for comfort. She laughed from the tingly feelings provided from the pain medication and the individual attention from Jeremiah.

"What's so funny, silly?" he had asked while laughing along with her.

"I feel funny," she replied.

"I bet. Those pain meds do wonders. That's why they only give you a handful with no refills," he added.

Thinking back, it just seemed sad how her thirteen-year-old self was trying to play house with a twenty-year-old man, how lonely she had been. Jeremiah had obviously seen her as a younger sister and had maintained beautiful boundaries. Losing his own younger sister to cancer when she was only ten years old, it had clearly fulfilled a void in his own life's journey to be so present for her back then. She was thankful for his example now, even though at the time, it had frustrated her to no end and caused her heart to ache.

She recalled the last 4th of July she would ever have at her grandparents' lakeside home. It had been the summer before high school when she was fourteen. The day had started cool and rainy but showed promises of warming up and seeing sunshine by noon. Dean, the oldest of the four neighbor kids up the street, came to see her alone. His siblings had gone to town with his mother to get groceries for the big barbecue Lillian looked forward to every year. Her grandfather always set off fireworks, and any neighbors who were home were always welcome. Dean and Lillian had gone together, alone to the sauna, to share the fears and excitement that high school would offer. The mixture of heat and hormones had led to her first kiss. He smelled of peanut butter and sweet sweat. The kiss was gentle and special. His soft, wet, warm tongue had entered her mouth, and she'd enjoyed the rhythmic movements as his lips devoured hers. She hadn't wanted it to end. She recalled feeling ecstatic from head to toe. She also hadn't forgotten that glimpse of a kind boy given to her that day.

"I know we live in two different worlds, Lil, but I will love you forever." He had held her in his warm arms, sweat dripping down their bodies, for several minutes of young, explorative kissing.

Chapter 11

Lillian had not been the only summer visitor to "God's Country," as the locals called it. Two other visitors had made a profound impact on her life that last summer. Twin sisters, Angela and Jessica, came sporadically from Wisconsin to visit their grandmother, who lived in the house to the north side of Lillian's grandparents. While Dean and his siblings offered safety and excitement through wild adventures of pretend play in the outdoors, Lillian had been convinced the twin sisters came only to torment and scar her. Her most vivid memory was an invitation to play hide-and-seek.

She could easily remember the day using all five of her senses—an exercise she now often facilitated with her therapy clients, to recall the smell, taste, sound, sight, and touch of memories. The smell of fresh blackberries and raspberries had been especially heightened that day, along with the freshly cut grass that she had helped her grandfather with earlier that morning. Mixing the blue and red berries together made a purple stain that remained on her fingertips and became her replacement for a lipstick if she held them to her lips and sucked while wiping back and forth just so. The taste of the berries had satisfied her hunger between breakfast and dinner. There was hardly time for lunch most days because there was so much exploring to do. The sounds Lillian readily recalled included the clucking laughter of the twins, in earnest preparation of a game, as they banged and clanged inside their grandmother's shed, as well as the rhythmic rapping of the pleated woodpeckers and the swishing flow of Lake Superior. The sights that stirred Lillian's memories were the most vivid—a lake view everywhere that had her imagining it was the closest vision of heaven on earth available. A perfect blend of nature, unlike any she had seen in the lower peninsula of the state, had made her stop and stare, even as a child. It was the combined beauty and peace of the woods on one side, with the never-ending lake on the other, that would always be etched in her soul.

But it was the touch of cool, soft grass under her feet, barefooted as usual, that transported her right back to the lakeside. Not having learned her lesson from that deep, open wound on her foot the summer before, she had headed out the back toward the dock that eventful day. She could almost feel the ridges of the healed scar against the cool grass, and it had made her smile. That scar was a reminder of a precious moment in time with Jeremiah.

The smooth rocks lining the pathway from the house to the sauna to the cottage had easily carried her to the stone dock, where she sat and stared out into the vast lake that appeared more as a calm, clear, endless ocean. She had been the neighborhood rock-skipping champion. The smooth rocks, so easy to find and hold just right between her first finger and thumb, had made it effortless for her to lean to the right, pull her arm back, and toss at the perfect angle. Her highest score was still engraved on the wooden beam in the corner of the cottage: Lil 27 skips, summer of… The year had been impossible to read; a piece of the wood was chipped off. The moment would have to stay commemorated without proof of a year. She had often challenged herself and skipped with her left hand, never able to come close to her dominant right-handed score.

"Ready!" the twins had hollered in unison at Lillian. The decision to trust and walk forward at that moment proved to be another building block in her journey to understand human nature, which eventually had driven her into the field of psychology. Angela, the oldest of the girls, by a whole 2 minutes, was bossier and more aggressive. No doubt she had probably shoved her sister aside and tied her up with the umbilical cord so she could travel through her mother's birth canal first, grown-up Lillian concluded. Angela had approached Lillian and told her to turn around and close her eyes. She had obeyed with little hesitation, desperate for bonding and friendship.

Angela had wrapped a scarf around Lillian's eyes and spun her around. It smelled like mummo—was it Chanel? She intertwined their hands, moist and warm.

"Trust me," she had whispered. Her breath was sweet and smelled of the berries Lillian used to tint her lips. The moment seemed to go in slow motion, but it could have only been thirty seconds, a minute at the most. Angela had led Lillian to the front of the shed.

"I'm going to take off the scarf. Keep your eyes closed and count to ten, then enter the shed; there is a surprise for you!" she had ordered. Lillian did what she was instructed and heard the twins laughing faintly from behind her, where they must have strategically chosen to stay out of the way but still enjoy the show.

"Eight, nine, ten…" Lillian had pulled down the scarf and wore it like a choker as she grabbed the shed door and pulled. A warm, shocking wetness overwhelmed her. She was blinded almost immediately and found it difficult to breath until she had managed to use the scarf to clear two small breathing holes for her nostrils. Covered in what she later discovered as brown paint, once she was able to open and wipe her eyes, Lillian stood frozen. Some drops of paint had fallen on Benji, her faithful shadow. Once the shock dissipated, her body had flushed with adrenaline, and she transitioned to flight. She had run back to her grandmother's property, alongside the front windows of the cottage that faced the lawn and the main house. In her hurry, she had completely forgotten about the badminton net she had asked her grandfather to set up that morning after mowing the lawn. She had run directly into the netting, with her nose as the first contact, causing her to jolt backwards and land hard on her back on the grass. A throbbing pain in her tailbone and a stinging pain washing over her face, Lillian had just looked up at the sky and broke into laughter. Through the laughter, an emotional explosion of anger cut in and had transformed the hilarity into uncontrollable sobbing. And there she remained—crying, hurting, betrayed.

Chapter 12

J eremiah, picking vegetables in his grandfather's garden next door, had heard Lillian wail and Benji bark. He leapt over the small creek dividing their property that hugged the southern wall of their sauna. Within seconds, he was standing over her.

"What happened, Lil?" he inquired, bending down. She had been embarrassed, and her sobs had made it impossible to articulate a sentence. He sat down in the grass, legs crossed, patiently waiting for her to calm down and talk. She could see him assessing the situation, as he took quick inventory of the evidence like a detective at a crime scene, which included brown paint on her head, face, and shoulders, netting marks pressed onto her face, and brown paint on the net that had been in front of her. Benji, flecked with drops of paint, had sat faithfully, watching Lillian and Jeremiah, waiting for the next move.

Jeremiah had looked over his right shoulder at the other neighbor's shed, where the door stood open, and a tipped paint can appeared to have been rigged above. He saw the brat twins, appropriately nicknamed by the neighborhood kids, peering from their grandmother's back porch with giant smiles on their faces. With a single scoop, he had gathered Lillian up carefully and headed to his back porch. Gently he maneuvered her over the creek using the man-made bridge he'd helped her grandfather fashion a few summers back. The bridge was like a structure out of a fairy tale that Lillian had had many a make-believe play session on over the years, including the long-awaited prince fantasy she had just lived through with Jeremiah.

"Come on, boy," Jeremiah prompted Benji to follow with a command and a whistle. He had gently placed her on a recliner porch chair and told her he would be right back. Returning with a bucket of clean, warm water, a washcloth, lemonade, and a first aid kit, he was prepared to address the superficial marks that were bleeding on her nose and chin. Not forgetting Benji, he had gone back inside and returned with a bowl of water for him. Jeremiah ran the hose right off the porch and cleaned the paint drops off Benji, giving Lillian a moment to settle. Like any good water-loving dog, the amiable dachshund had welcomed his spontaneous bath. Rubbing Benji down with a towel and wrapping him like a burrito, Jeremiah then rejoined Lillian back on the porch with her swaddled fur baby.

"The twins?" Testing the atmosphere and Lillian's readiness to process the event, Jeremiah had asked an obvious question to which he already knew the answer. Lillian had nodded slowly, still sobbing, her eyes swollen and staring off into the distance. Jeremiah looked out at the lake and smiled.

"One more injury, girl, and I'm considering wrapping you in bubble wrap," he quipped, hoping to lighten the mood. "Seriously, I'm thinking I should switch my major to pre-med to prepare myself for what's in store next summer," he had added. Lillian's sobs slowed down as she took deep belly breaths in and out through her nose, practicing her relaxation breathing yet again.

"I trusted them; I hate them," she had whispered through clenched teeth, barely opening her lips.

"Hey, I hear you. But hate requires a lot of energy, Lil. Maybe put that energy into praying for them?" Jeremiah replied. Her head snapped up and she stared at him in disbelief.

"Well, I think that's about the hardest thing God expects us to do. Pray for our enemies, ha! I'd rather pour honey on them and leave them in the woods for the black bears!" she had snapped back. Jeremiah's eyebrows shot up, but he had nodded in understanding.

"Woah, that's dark, girl! But I also hear you. It is the hardest thing. It's kind of easy to love the lovable, right?" he questioned. Lillian continued looking into Jeremiah's eyes and remained silent, but in her mind, she had said, *Like I love you.*

"If you can believe this, people who hurt you are actually hurting. If you can remember that little secret, it can help you realize it's not personal, so praying for them is a little easier. Pray that their hearts soften, so they can know and feel the love of God in their lives. Pray their hurt gets healed, so they will stop hurting others," Jeremiah offered. Lillian had allowed Jeremiah to blot her face with the washcloth and sat still as he placed ointment on her nose and chin.

"Are you able to wash your hair in the sauna shower, so you won't drag paint through the house? The sooner the better." he urged. Lillian, with her young, tender heart racing, wanted to respond, *No, I need you to come in the shower and help me and kiss me all over,* but instead, she had simply nodded.

Chapter 13

It was not until that evening during dinner that Lillian had realized that Jeremiah was not the only one who had witnessed her traumatic event. Lillian was dipping a chunk of her warm pasty, a pot pie without the pot stuffed with meat and vegetables, in ketchup when her mother asked what on earth had happened to her face. She was briefly excited that her mother had noticed. She was usually too consumed with her own thoughts to notice Lillian might be having any important ones of her own.

"Lillian ran into the badminton net after the twins poured paint all over her face," her grandmother had answered before she could explain herself. Lillian had been shocked and furious. Her grandmother had not been in the main house at the time but was sitting in the back corner of the cottage, knitting in her rocking chair. She had had a front row seat for the entire event.

Lillian pounded her fist on the table and stood up. Benji barked. She had so much to say but remained mute. Adult Lillian was able to advocate for herself when reflecting on the core memory. I should have said, "What kind of a grandmother sees something like that and doesn't say anything or make sure I'm okay? What's wrong with you?" Perhaps surprised she had reacted with a firm fist pound, usually so quiet and eager to please, both her mother and father looked up from their plates.

"Lil-li-an!" their voices had rung out in unison. She had stormed out of the kitchen and headed down the backyard hill, past the sauna, beyond the cottage, and to the shoreline; Benji had followed, innocently ready for the next escapade. An important epiphany took place in that moment as she sat on the dock and stared at the calm lake, fighting back tears. Something wasn't right with her family tree.

Deeply sad and frustrated, she had rolled off the dock in her clothes, careful to avoid letting the water slap her raw and stinging face injuries from earlier that day, and she had floated on her back in the lake. Looking up at the clear sky, already freezing, she wondered if she just laid there and allowed herself to float out beyond the shore, who would notice first? Who would look for her? Who would rescue her? She was sure it would be Jeremiah. She would like that, and so she was actually tempted to test her theory. Hearing Benji bark, feeling left behind no doubt and ready to jump in after her, she had brought herself back to reality. Also, deciding that she did not trust anyone else to take care of him like she could if she did float away—except Jeremiah, of course—but then what would happen when he had to go back to school? Talking herself out of it, and not wanting to worry her faithful companion, she flipped back to her stomach and swam back to the shallow. Gaining her ground and walking up to the shore, she had greeted her little friend.

"I won't leave you, boy," she assured him, as Benji greeted her with a wagging tail and licks. "I was just thinking and pouting." Turning to face the water, she sat down and looked behind her right shoulder to see Jeremiah sitting on the large porch with his grandfather, both with a beer in hand. She saw his mouth moving as he smiled and appeared to be enjoying the conversation he was having. Jeremiah glanced towards her and gave a casual wave. She smiled and waved back while shivering, mentally commanding him to join her but remaining silent. She began to take off her wet clothes, stripping down to the bathing suit she had always worn under outfits for spontaneous trips to the sauna or lake. She looked over again, hoping he had noticed, but he was gone.

Within a minute, Jeremiah walked up behind her, startling her. The surprise sent her heart racing, in a good way. He offered her a large, warm beach towel.

"Hey, I noticed you seemed to take an impulsive swim in your clothes. Thought you might need this. Just pulled it out of the dryer," he explained, speaking just a little too slowly and slightly slurred, as he wrapped the towel around her like a queen's robe and moved a little unsteadily to sit down on a smooth rock next to her, beer still in hand. "Mind if I join you?" he asked, slightly misjudging the height of the rock and nearly thumping down on the surface. She shook her head yes as her body trembled, and her lips turned a light shade of blue. In her head, the answer had sounded more like, *You can join me for the rest of my life.*

"You okay? That was a little clumsy there," Lillian commented.

"That WAS a little clumsy, wasn't it? So, what's up? How is your face doing? Do you need more ointment?" he asked, intentionally turning her chin to see the markings and to do a full inspection of his work. Jeremiah brushed a piece of her hair off her face so he could see better, sending pleasant chills down her spine. The butterflies that usually took residence in her stomach were lower now.

"It stings, but I'm okay. The ointment is still there; I made sure not to get my face in the water. Can I have a taste of your beer?" she asked with chattering teeth.

"No, I'm not contributing to the delinquency of a minor. Your parents would never forgive me," Jeremiah replied as he laughed and rubbed her back up and down to create some warmth.

"Jeremiah!" his grandfather's voice carried over from the porch. They both looked back to see his grandfather shaking his head in disapproval. Jeremiah's face flushed as he removed his hand. Lillian was confused.

"What was that about?" she asked.

"Nothing, what were we saying?" he urged her to continue.

"Not true, my parents wouldn't care. If they even noticed at all. Besides, once during communion, I went into the wine line, instead of the grape juice line, and no one ever noticed then," Lillian insisted.

"Is that right? What did you think?" Jeremiah challenged.

"It was disgusting, but I liked the tingles I felt when I drank it," she responded.

"Beer is kind of disgusting too, but I guess that's why people drink, for the tingles." He looked down at the beer in his hand for a second and then poured his remaining dark liquid out into the rocks and continued, "Just a little advice. When you're in college—and hopefully twenty-one, might I add—start with wine coolers, something moderate, and be careful. You don't want to get alcohol poisoning. Never leave your drink unattended and then go back to it; there are bad guys out there who put drugs in girls' drinks and then try to take advantage of them. You know what I mean about take advantage, right? You must be so careful, Lil. Ugh, now I will worry about you in high school and college. Promise you will be careful?"

"I know what you mean. I will be careful," Lillian reassured him and nodded.

"Where were you floating off to?" he asked, changing the subject.

Slow to formulate a response, she finally answered, "I was going to float away to a place where I would be seen AND heard, but I didn't want to leave Benji." *Or you,* her mind whispered.

"How come you feel that way? What's going on?" he questioned as his thinking wrinkle emerged between his eyebrows.

"Thank you for always seeing me and hearing me, Jeremiah," was all she offered, minimizing her feelings and not elaborating.

"Hey, always! You deserve to be seen and heard. I know sometimes adults don't do or say the right things, Lil, but God always sees and hears you. Don't forget that. Don't forget to talk to Him."

Chapter 14

Lillian had found herself in the sauna more often that summer. She even took a beer now and then from the sauna fridge. The adults stocked them to have while they sweated out the toxins and decompressed. She couldn't imagine that any of the tuned-out adults in her life kept count of the beers and shared the tallies with each other. Any empties she had were placed in her grandfather's empty bottle bin that he returned to the store regularly for a few dollars to put toward the next grocery order.

She also took to leaving the curtain open, not shutting it as her grandmother had instructed her to do. Perhaps it was her way to protest the adults in her life, or just take a stance for her own independence. Or maybe she just hoped Jeremiah would wander by, look in, and notice her in a different way, now blossoming with a woman's figure. Maybe even Dean would visit with more kisses, she had imagined with excitement as she purposefully sat naked on the top bench watching sweat drops race down her now full breasts and hips. The feeling had been invigorating and led her to the beginning of self-exploration.

Chapter 15

She never knew that Jeremiah had wandered by, just once. Going against every fiber in his body telling him it was wrong, he looked. He lingered. He imagined. His grandfather must have sensed his inner conflict. Just a few days later, he'd confronted his grandson about the closeness between the two. He was kind but direct when he stressed the need he felt to protect them both. He explained to Jeremiah that since he was older, and in a position of authority, he was held to a higher standard, both legally and morally.

"Four years from now, maybe. Right now, remember she's a child, Jeremiah. Get it out of your head. I know we're tucked away up here in a magical, fairy tale community, but even here, it's a crime. You understand?" he asked, concerned. Jeremiah understood. He really just needed someone to say it out loud and remind him that he was accountable. It's what he would have wanted for his sister, he would continually tell himself. So, that was that.

Chapter 16

Lillian's grandfather had filled her days with berry-picking, lawn-mowing, and garage-tinkering. He rigged a clothesline from the back deck to a tree. Her fingers were sore from pinching clothes pins on and off, allowing nature to dry the garments. She enjoyed this chore. She sang songs while scattering the vibrant colors down the line, so when the wind blew through them, it created a beautiful kaleidoscope. Nights resonated with bonfires. The evening festivities only lasted for as long as they could stand the eerie sight of bats diving low overhead, hunting insects. In fact, the bats had usually been the sign that it was time to put the fire out and go to bed. The gatherings ended in sprints to the house, heads covered in shirts or blankets for fear of bats getting caught in your hair. Mornings were welcomed with the smell of Pannukakku, a baked Finnish pancake served with fresh jam made from the hours of berry-picking up by the main gravel road.

Her last core memory, before her summer in the north had ended, began as any other day. Her grandfather took the neighbor Dean, his brother, and their father, as well as Lillian's own father out on his boat for a man's fishing day. Her grandfather had strict fishing rules: no radio offering access to the world; they had to fish like their ancestors. Lillian had been busy with her mother, grandmother, and Dean's sisters preparing sides to have for a big fish fry they'd make with the fresh catch they anticipated the men would bring back. The refrigerator was packed with pasties just in case the fishing expedition was unsuccessful. As the hour for the men to return drew near, a thick, dense fog rolled in. It was eerie and unlike any fog Lillian had ever seen. The chatter that started among the women grew, laced with fear and worry that the fishermen would not be able to see the shore. Refusing to leave their destiny to the legacy of all the past shipwreck victims of the Great Lakes, her grandmother rallied the neighbors for help.

Jeremiah, who had stayed behind to fix shingles on his grandfather's roof before another harsh winter, quickly joined the rescue mission. He suggested creating some loud noise to help the returning crew find their way. Organizing four cars and three pickup trucks at the property midway on the dead-end street, they lined up in the grass along the rocky shore. Each owner had honked their horn, projecting a blast of sound in an attempt to lead her grandfather's boat to safety. After almost two hours of honking, the boat cleared from behind the wall of fog. The rescue party began cheering and clapping as they grabbed the ropes and tied the boat down at the neighbor's dock.

Lillian saw exhaustion and relief on her grandfather's face. He looked older. One by one, as the men exited the boat, they ran to their significant others in relief and gratitude. Dean's brother ran to his chocolate Labrador, barking excitedly to see his best friend, and Dean ran to Lillian.

"I thought I'd never see you again," he whispered. Welcoming his embrace, Lillian placed her chin on his shoulder and nestled his neck. She made eye contact with Jeremiah in the distance, who smiled and winked. He had been encouraging her affection for a boy her own age. She had not been able to ignore the little voice inside her head saying, *I wish I was nestled against your neck, Jeremiah Heikkinen.* Lillian, thankful for Dean's return and clearly expressed attraction to her, enjoyed another round of tender and passionate kisses that evening. Cuddling under a sky splattered with bright, endless stars and a full moon, she realized that when she closed her eyes, it was Jeremiah's lips that enveloped hers.

Chapter 17

As an adult woman and seasoned therapist, Lillian reflected on that impactful childhood memory. The visualization of the boat coming through the thick fog felt symbolic, like the veil or temple curtain being torn when Jesus died on the cross. Her father had shared the biblical event as a guest pastor in church one Sunday that summer. It had caught her attention, but it really meant nothing to her as a fourteen-year-old girl. It was just another story from an overwhelming book of stories that her father had seemed to study passionately. It must have struck her, though, because she listened to that account, even though she pretended not to as she doodled on the church bulletin. So many times since then, it had come back to her and she often reflected on that veil.

There were countless times her clients felt a veil lift right in the middle of a session when they discovered a deeper understanding of themselves or their circumstance. Then there is also the symbolic fog of the enemy, the dark force in the world, that creates its own veil of worry, fear, and confusion, Lillian recognized. Her role continued to be to intentionally facilitate a clear path of understanding. Sometimes that clarity came with a gentle whisper or an open-ended question, and sometimes with a leaf-blower blazing full speed. Unfortunately, she admitted to herself, she continued to live behind her own stubborn, foggy smokescreen of worry and confusion. Maybe it was the gale force of a hurricane that she needed to clear it out once and for all.

When the near-tragic boat event happened that summer, she had had no idea that it would be her last summer in the north and she would never see Dean again. In fact, she would only see Jeremiah one more time after that. For years, she held an overwhelming hope that when she turned eighteen, Jeremiah would be waiting for her, down on one knee, to present her with an engagement ring. But now she knew, that was not to be.

Chapter 18

After the *accident,* her whole life suddenly ceased to exist as she had known it. *Accident* was the term her father had coined and continued to use to this day, she reflected critically. It had taken years for Lillian to realize that it was his own denial that had prompted her father to call her mother's intentional ingestion of three different saved bottles of painkillers an "accident." Hoarded pills, from three separate root canals, taken only two days after they had arrived home from their long summer vacation, couldn't possibly be categorized as anything accidental. But he was a pastor and pastors' wives do not take their own lives. Just like pastors don't engage in adultery or manipulate scared young girls into making an appointment at an abortion clinic. Pastors lived lives of service to God and God's lost people. They obeyed God's laws.

Today, walking back down the streets of ancient Spanish St. Augustine, lined with religious structures, Lillian shook her head in exasperation. She no longer believed in religious absolutes of any kind.

At age fourteen, Lillian's naivety had been bulldozed when her mother died by suicide and Lillian lost the wonderment of God. Then at the age of eighteen, after being manipulated, misled, and abandoned by a man of God, she lost her faith. She didn't lose faith that God existed; there was proof of Him all around. She lost faith in His goodness, couldn't understand His love, and wasn't sure that He was even *for* her. She realized, with a sense of guilt, that no one is safe from the temptations of the flesh, despite their title or calling. Lillian defensively shoved the memories away, back into their compartment, and focused her thoughts back on her therapy sessions with Hannah. Hannah's story was so redemptive and yet always baffling to her.

Chapter 19

Hannah had lived for the stories and pictures brought to her by her friends upon their returns from vacations and escapades. Right next to her bed, the postcard from Hawaii that her friend Brooke had sent her the previous spring was push-pinned. She would hold the flashlight on it sometimes when she couldn't sleep.

"What do you imagine, lying there with your light shining?" Lillian had inquired.

"I imagine lying on the beach or snorkeling alongside a sea turtle in the clear ocean or ordering room service while I read a book for fun, out on my hotel balcony, the sun radiating down on me," Hannah excitedly responded.

Hannah was the oldest of five children, with a stay-at-home mom, and a dad who worked nine to five, and they always had just enough for their modest lifestyle. Just enough money, food, and gas, but nothing more and nothing less. That was her life, the monotony that made her feel like she just bounced around the confines of her home, that drove her to Olympic-paced bike rides and endless hours hidden away in the back of her walk-in closet. She had spent endless hours reading numerous chapters in her mother's dusty coffee table books about faraway places. She'd cut out images from old *National Geographic* magazines stored away in the attic to make vision boards of colorful locations. And she'd contemplated her existence, feeling like she would surely go mad or die if something exciting didn't hit her hard in her face or whisk her away one day.

It was obvious to Hannah that some people were marked for greatness—wealth, popularity, looks—while others couldn't catch a break and were plagued with illness, financial struggles, and despair. Then there was the desolate land in the middle, her world, where there was no greatness or tragedy.

"Which way would you rather have it?" Lillian had often pushed in sessions. "What are you gaining or missing either way?" Hannah struggled to define a clear answer. How could she determine something she had never experienced? Those she knew with the mark of greatness had often been doomed to crash and burn at some point, she had reasoned to Lillian. Their spectacular world seemed to spiral out of control, too good to be true for very long.

Take Daniel, for example, a popular guy in her school, with a full-ride football scholarship to the University of Florida. He had landed himself in court-ordered rehab after serving jail time because his wealth and popularity had bought him an invitation to endless parties featuring toxic amounts of alcohol and drugs. The combination of stimulants and depressants had successfully rescued him from his high-pressured reality. Tragically, that combination also had him driving recklessly down highway US 1 as his teammate clumsily fumbled with his iPhone in the passenger seat. As Daniel had turned onto West King Street, with music blasting, he'd been unable to focus on or react to the ten-year-old boy crossing the road in front of him. He had hit and killed the boy instantly. That innocent boy, named Jace, was walking home from an errand to get fever medicine for his baby sister. The news anchor explained that he had dreams of playing college basketball always bouncing around in his head. His basketball talent was supposed to get him to the NBA, the big money, and it was supposed to get his family out of poverty, Hannah had explained.

"So then, what about his family?" Hannah stressed. "They are perfect examples of the other kind of people who cannot seem to catch a break."

Jace's welfare-dependent, single mother had just buried her eldest son six months earlier after he had been violently shot in her living room—a random gang initiation drive-by. The stolen Smith and Wesson that had taken his life erased his existence by way of a 9mm round lodged in his left lung, as Jace's mom had sat two feet away, nursing her fifth child. That unfortunate infant's tiny mouth was barely able to suck any sustenance from her mother's nearly-empty milk vessel—poverty at its worst. Their front window, too expensive to fix, still marked the memory of the tragedy—a cheap memorial, rigged with cardboard and duct tape to keep out the bugs and rain. Throwing up her hands in frustration, Hannah added, "Now that mother must prepare to bury her second son, an unfair and cruel sentence, given to her from a God she cannot see, hear, or touch. Her son's dreams of basketball are smeared on the pavement, diluted by his blood and the cherry-flavored medicine, all mixing together. Just an eerie scarlet stain on the pavement…maybe for years to come," she added.

Hannah confessed to Lillian that she still got chills every time she passed the floral cross placed at the side of the road which marked the young boy's place of death, the place he took his final breath while doing an unselfish act. That place commemorated the location where two completely different worlds, greatness and despair, came crashing together.

Chapter 20

Lillian couldn't help but marvel at how full of questions and thoughts about life Hannah had been. She had so many questions about the convoluted unfairness of it. Her mother hadn't ever talked to her about things in-depth, too wrapped up in diapers, soap operas, and budget-friendly dinners. Her father would give her a smile and a pat on the head when he walked through the door, but he had always changed the subject if Hannah brought up anything other than the daily humdrum. Hannah had speculated that any deep conversation would have tipped the tedious scale and caused her father to have to think beyond his nine-to-five routine and the sports channels.

Racing thoughts zoomed through Hannah's mind, tormenting her sanity and poise. *There has to be more!* the voice-tormentors screamed to her. But she dared not ask the question out loud for fear of being told that she was wrong, that there WASN'T actually more. She had dreaded that if she verbalized that thought, a great voice would respond, *You live, you die, the end. Some are great, some aren't, most suffer. There is nothing more, Hannah, so get over it.* At least if she kept her fears to herself, she could pretend that there was a hope for more. She had only spoken her fear out loud to Lillian, trusting her to keep it from erupting into reality by locking it away in her therapy filing cabinet.

Lillian recognized the existential storm inside of Hannah. Bright and inquisitive, her concerns weren't a surprise, and Lillian had known she needed to steer their sessions towards self-awareness and purposeful living. Lillian had to walk a tightrope of sensitivity regarding Hannah's cultural and spiritual values, which were still impressionable, not yet ingrained.

By nature, Hannah had done everything she was told. She was a good girl who submitted to authority and never rocked the boat. Although she was already into young adulthood when Lillian started working with her, Hannah remained within her childhood home. As surrogate mother to her younger four brothers, two sets of twins, she filled in when her mother was sick or just needed alone time. She had helped stabilize her family, tackling more than one person's share of chores around the house. She was beyond her years in wisdom and bored with the things her friends at school were consumed by. The next social event, new movie release, or the latest sale on designer clothes and sunglasses had held no interest for her. She realized that an outfit would be worn at a party, to get noticed by the hot guy or girl, and the rest, as they say, stays in Vegas. She would have nothing to do with any of it. Oh, how she had longed for someone to just hurl something amazing at her.

Hannah had deliberately worked hard in school and kept her commitments to family, friends, and babysitting clients. She had been a freshman at the local community college with an undecided major, just chipping away at prerequisites while she lived at home. Her passions were not yet exposed. But she continued to breathe through the boredom and push on because she was convinced that life had to be about more than what it was offering her then and there. Her innate curiosity and frustration never dissipated. It was like her soul waited to discover a purpose...an ordinary girl looking for something extraordinary to live for.

Chapter 21

For Hannah, that extraordinary thing did happen for her one day. She told Lillian she would never forget that strangely cold and dreary day that the something amazing she was waiting for arrived in the mail. It had been a Saturday. She remembered preparing to walk up to the corner to grab a coffee before buckling down and finishing her research paper for Philosophy class, due Monday. She had tried to sneak out, because if there was any inclination that she was escaping, she had four little shadows begging her to take them. She did not mind the tagalongs. She loved the twins with her whole heart, but with their ever-constant clinging, she couldn't sort out her own identity. Always this source of life for them, it had caused her to forget that she was actually an individual with one heartbeat, not five.

On her way out, she checked the mail and noticed an 11x14 white FedEx envelope addressed to her. Little had she known that what was inside would change her life forever. As she recounted the story to Lillian, she marveled at how many countless hours she had wasted filled with frustration from being ordinary, and the answers had just shown up in a package from across the world. Hannah had forgotten about the coffee and the unusual outdoor chill as she sat on their outside deck and stared at her package.

As it turned out, that was the day life had offered her more, and not just answers to her questions, but answers to who she was, and why she was. Hannah had opened the seal slowly and precisely. Inside was a folded letter that simply read *To Hannah* lying on top of a book. She carefully unfolded the letter, her hands trembling, anticipating something special, just for her. She had been desperate for anything that would be greater than writing a contemporary philosophy paper on capital punishment. *To kill or not to kill? An eye for an eye?* The questions had bobbled around in her head.

Chapter 22

She brought the letter to their session to read out loud to Lillian. She paused between paragraphs to process her thoughts, feelings, and behaviors. She walked Lillian through the whole experience. The letter read:

My dearest Hannah,

So long I have meant to write you, so many words to say to you, my dear granddaughter. How old you must be getting. How beautiful you must be! I hope this package finds you first. I fear that your mother will throw it away if she opens this. Please, Miriam, if you have intercepted this 'gift,' please allow Hannah to hear what I have to say and decide for herself if she wants to accept it.

I am so sorry that my life's work took me away from you at such a young age, Hannah. I have been so caught up in the mission field that I left my family behind. Now, as I have chosen to give up fighting the disease that has been eating away at my old body, I am too sick to come home. So, I beg for your forgiveness from afar and pray that I am not too late. I have come to realize that if I die without sharing what I know with you, my eldest, precious granddaughter, nothing I have done over here, all these years, will have mattered to me.

Hannah could hardly contain herself as she read. Her mother had never talked about her grandma. She assumed her grandma had died. Looking down at the letter, she imagined an old woman, malnourished, lying in some mud hut, scribbling this letter with every last bit of energy she had. Hannah flipped the package over to look at the return address: Africa. She ran inside, tripping on the twins' shoes as she leapt up the stairs, clearing three at a time, to get to her room. Her legs burned by the time she reached the top. She locked the door. Hannah studied her world map that was pinned to her wall and marked with different colors. There were countries circled that she intended to visit one day and countries crossed out that she didn't really care to go to, as well as oceans highlighted that she wanted to swim in. And then there were the states outlined that she planned to drive through when she got out of her uninspiring town. Her finger traced the map, searching for the location of where the parcel had arrived from. Searching the continent of Africa, Hannah found the country of Kenya, just under Egypt, on the border of the Red Sea. Her grandmother lay in the desert plains of Africa helping the Kenyans?! She retreated into her closet. She read on.

Hannah, you are alive for a very important purpose! How confused and frustrated you must be if no one has explained this to you yet. If your parents have never talked to you about this, I blame myself. They rejected this extraordinary message after the tragic death of your grandfather here on the mission field, when I told them that I wasn't coming home.

So there was a tragedy in our family! A tragedy and a grandmother never spoken of, living in a foreign country with a cryptic message for me! Hannah thought excitedly. She blinked hard and slow several times, hoping the letter would remain in her hands when she opened her eyes, anticipating it was a dream or fantasy, not quite able to believe the words she was reading—not yet.

You were created by the Lord, our God, who is the Creator of heaven and earth. He has many names! Each name describes who God is and what God does. Some call him Abba or Adonai; others call him Father, Elohim, or Yahweh. He is the King of kings, the Truth, the Way, the Beginning and the End. He created you in His image, Hannah. You are His daughter; He has an extraordinary plan for your life! If you accept Him, by first accepting His Son, Jesus, you will be adopted into His royal family. You will be filled with His Holy Spirit. When your time on this earth is done, you will live forever in eternity with Him. Grandpa is there and I know I will be there soon too! I regret that I stayed away from you all of these years and am now relying on paper and pen to do what I should have done in person, years ago. I've been such a fool. I can only hope you'll honor my last wishes and hear me out.

Hannah, God sent His Son, Jesus, to this earth over 2,000 years ago. Born from a virgin, he lived among the people, performed miracles, healed the sick, and raised the dead. He walked with sinners. He walked with those society felt were insignificant and unworthy.

"God's Son walked the earth with ordinary people, like me," Hannah shared. Lillian listened.

He was fully God and fully man. He did not sin, He was perfect flesh, and when the Father God chose, at the age of 33, Jesus died on a cross, nails piercing his hands and feet, His perfect blood shed for you as a sacrifice! His earthly mission was complete. Jesus died for your sins so you could be reconciled with the Father. But, Hannah, it didn't stop there. He rose from the dead three days later, His torn body, beautiful and restored, left with only the scars from the nails

and the piercing of the sword in His side. More than anything,
He wants to have a personal relationship with you. Pray in
Jesus' name and ask for God's will to be done in your life.

Hannah had flipped the letter over on her lap, incredulous. Her long-lost grandmother contacted her on her death bed, with an extraordinary story about God and her own destiny. She wasn't sure if she was skeptical, excited, or irritated. For a moment, she wasn't even sure she was going to read the rest of the letter.

"I realized I was just holding my breath and sitting there," she explained.

"Tell me more," Lillian encouraged and nodded. Hannah continued to share that the ticking of the clock echoed in her ears, punctuating her indecision. Then a shriek in the distance and what sounded like a stampede of footsteps roaring past her door jerked her back to her ordinary reality and she swiftly flipped the letter back over and continued to read.

I know this is a lot to take in all at one time. It's even a lot
for me to ask you to consider, having not made the time
to prioritize our relationship in person. But, please, take a
deep breath and keep reading, child. What an extraordinary
plan He has in store for you! Don't let my foolish choices
come between you and our God. Enclosed in this package
is my personal Bible. It is my most precious possession and
I'm sending it to you. This is God's Living and perfect Word!
I have highlighted and marked specific scriptures for you,
Hannah, to get you started. Oh, that I could be there with
you right now! But, listen, this is how you become a child
in God's family. It's so important and yet so simple. First,
speak out loud to the Father God and tell Him that you
accept that you are a sinner, unable and unworthy to save
yourself, no matter how many good things you do or say.
Second, believe that Jesus is God's Son who died for you, He
sacrificed His life for yours, and the only way to be with the

Father is through His Son, Jesus Christ. And lastly, confess with your mouth that you believe that Jesus Christ is Lord, and ask Him into your heart! With this simple prayer, the Holy Spirit will come upon you and dwell in you. He will guide you and give you wisdom. Then tell someone. It's so important to tell someone—to confess your connection with God to others. Again, I mourn that I am not there to be your shepherd. It SHOULD be me! Go to someone mature in the faith so they may walk with you and guide you. Be diligent. Start looking and let them help you build your faith. Then, when you are ready, go to someone else who is new to the faith, and shepherd them just as you have been shepherded. You should always have one hand following and one hand guiding. Oh, Hannah, such a message as this should be in person, face-to-face, and I am so sorry that I am not there with you. I pray you have an open heart and mind to receive what I am telling you. I pray that you will accept God's gift of love and grace, which is undeserved favor, and claim your royal inheritance as his daughter. It is important to go to God in prayer every day, several times a day, to stay close to Him, in constant conversation, as a best friend.

But, Hannah, beware. There is a dark side to this glory—an enemy. He roams around like a hungry beast, a lurking lion, tempting people to turn from God and His truth, tempting people to get wrapped up in earthly desires. His name is Lucifer, or Satan. He is a fallen angel with an evil army that was cast out of heaven by God. He is the father of lies; he deceives. He reminds people of their sins and drags them down into the pits of shame and guilt. He uses our feelings of unworthiness as proof that we are worthless. You must remember that your worth is through Jesus, who is inside you, not anything you've done or haven't done. It's not about works. God doesn't withhold blessings if you don't do works. Jesus did the work, and He is your worth. God can protect you from the evil schemes. Grow strong in God's knowledge, child. Read the pages of my Bible that teach of God's armor in Ephesians, a book in the New Testament. It is in the second half of the Bible. Seek out people to help you understand it more clearly and don't forget to give the gift of this Truth to your brothers. Pray for your parents that our God will soften their hearts and open their minds once again to this message. You have been chosen, Hannah! You may feel too young for such a task, but God's love, grace, and strength are sufficient. Time is running out. All must hear this message and be given an opportunity to accept Jesus. Those who reject Him will be judged and spend an eternity in a place called hell, with the evil one. Nothing but misery and pain exist there, eternal separation from God.

I know my time on this earth is almost over. I have been working for so long sharing this message with God's lost people in many foreign countries. I should have taken the time to make sure my own precious family understood it. Now, with my body too weak to travel, I see my mistake all too late. But I am prepared to go home to my Creator, where there is no pain or age, or poor judgment. Again, child, I cannot express how sorry I am that I did not make it back to you before my body wore down. I love you, Hannah. I can only pray I will run and worship with you in paradise one day. Please take all of this in, and read it however many times you need, until you can grasp a piece of it. If you accept this gift, Hannah, you will know love, peace, joy, purpose, and so much more! You really are extraordinary—the daughter of a King, created for a specific purpose! Stand strong in knowing Jesus died for you! Now go discover a strong voice and purposeful life for Him!

Your loving Grandmother.

Chapter 23

Hannah told Lillian she remembered sitting there, overwhelmed, tears welling in her eyes, unable to move, barely able to breathe, yet shaking almost uncontrollably. She was dizzy and could easily feel her heart racing, endorphins coursing through her body, giving her a rush. She had flopped back, flat on her back.

"The daughter of a King?" she repeated over and over. Then there was also the tragic death of a grandfather she felt desperate to hear more about. There was also the extraordinary life of a grandmother who she barely knew had existed and was convinced was not even alive. But then there was also that talk of a purpose and an inheritance.

"A purpose for me?" She had spoken the words out loud to consider them, to breathe them into the air and possibly give them life. She knew about God—who didn't, these days? But all the other implicit information the letter had delivered was a lot to swallow. She confessed to Lillian how confused, overwhelmed, frightened, and yet excited she had been. Not wanting the possibility of the gift to escape, she debated. It was incredible news, news that the more she thought about it, had to have been the news she'd been waiting for. The hope that she had been clutching onto had been more of a thread than a rope. But as thin and frail as it was, it helped her recognize the possibilities in what her grandmother had described. She realized she wanted to believe it. She wanted to try. And she wanted it to all be true. So, with a childlike faith, eager to accept all that her grandmother was offering her, Hannah accepted Jesus Christ as her personal Lord and Savior. Right there, in her private prison, in her closet, on an ordinary day, Hannah, an average girl no more, claimed her inheritance as the daughter of a King. Even though excitement and hope had filled her soul, she had no idea how extraordinary her faith journey would be or how instrumental it would be in bringing to fruition how truly exceptional she was.

Chapter 24

Lillian recalled how Hannah's experience had not ended with her declaration of faith. Months later, after the red tape of passports, airline tickets, and travel arrangements, Hannah had made it to the village where her failing grandmother lay, days before she would take her final breath on earth. Tucked safely away in a page of the Bible, Hannah's grandmother had sent a check containing the remainder of her life savings for her granddaughter. That check had provided the means for Hannah to make the trip, flights from Jacksonville to Atlanta, to Amsterdam to Nairobi to Kisumu, then a drive South to Kisii. She had been miraculously accompanied by her mother, who found forgiveness and peace in her once-rigid heart, through the tender approach of her daughter and the beautiful gift crafted by her mother. Hannah had specifically prayed that God would soften her mother's heart, and He did. With that forgiveness came a blossoming balance within Hannah's dysfunctional family. A much more present mother emerged, allowing Hannah to just be a daughter and a sibling, instead of a surrogate parent.

Sitting at her grandmother's bedside in Africa, Hannah and her mother had reaffirmed their acceptance of Jesus, with a prayer, hand-in-hand, three generations forming a circle of hope. They had both been baptized in a body of water, in the village of Kisii, while her grandmother watched. Hannah had been quick to point out to Lillian that the submersion of their bodies had symbolized the death of self, and the coming up out of the water symbolized a resurrection of a new life in Christ.

"A family, once ripped apart by anger, bitterness, and grief, was reconciled; a generational curse was broken!" she had said joyfully. "And so our three different stories remain intertwined—one who was lost but now found, one whose purpose on the earth had been fulfilled, and one whose time has just begun; brought together by a desire for more, and a love for Jesus."

Lillian could now see how Hannah had taken the gift offered from God through her grandmother. She had accepted the passing of the baton—a life of missionary work. But her call to the mission field had not taken her far away from home like it did her grandmother. Instead of foreign countries and distant lands, it had been clear to her that her purpose and calling would begin within her own home. Her own flesh and blood would come first, she had assured Lillian. She had vowed not to make the same foolish mistake her grandmother had confessed to her. Instead, as she gained knowledge and wisdom, she reached out to the students and faculty at her college, and upon graduation, her mission field became the neighborhood across Highway, US 1, down West King Street. Now she spent her days walking past that "floral cross" and over that "scarlet stain," where the life of that young mother and many much like her remained unchanged. She had recognized the lost people, stagnant, stuck in cycles of despair. Hannah, while clenching her grandmother's Bible and claiming her birthright as a princess, continued to bring a message of hope and glimpses of an invisible God. The King of kings was brought to sight, sound, and touch, by a young girl with a clear commitment. Hannah had found her extraordinary purpose and already began to make Kingdom impacts in her small corner of the world, one day and one step at a time.

Lillian realized that her time and work with Hannah had offered the young girl a safe haven for her to express her feelings and sort through things, but Hannah's transformation was more likely the work of God. Lillian had long ago accepted her calling to be an encourager and she met people where they were, but the real work was done when her clients gave up control and surrendered to something greater than themselves. She was just a seed planter. Lillian recognized that truth despite her own struggle with her own relationship and understanding of God.

"I hope you have a personal relationship with Jesus, Ms. Lillian. It's all that matters." Hannah's voice had dropped almost to a whisper as she leaned in, looking at Lillian intentionally during her discharge session.

"Thank you, Hannah. I'm so glad that you have found your purpose. You have done great work and I see the joy it has brought into your life. I wish you the best." Lillian smiled like a good, neutral therapist. She had not wanted the session to become about her instead of the client.

"I will pray for you, Ms. Lillian," Hannah had whispered as she impulsively wrapped her arms around Lillian on her way out the door. The impulsive act had filled Lillian with unanticipated warmth and compassion, causing her to gulp back a surge of emotion.

Chapter 25

As Lillian found her way back to her Spanish-style stucco home, Leo's tail began to wag, and his pace picked up at the smell of the familiar.

"Yes, boy, we're home!" she declared. *Home*, she ruminated, felt more and more like a house fallen short these days. She loved the house she and Joshua had bought and decorated together. Their love for South Florida and the Spanish influence reflected in their orange-tiled floors, often sprinkled with sand, that neither one of them stressed about sweeping. Having sand under their toes reminded them of the beauty of the beach, which was a big part of their love story.

A Jardin De Flores hand-painted Mexican Talavera backsplash covered the kitchen and bathrooms, combined with Spanish-influenced artwork in every room. The house had more windows than wall space. That was a main selling point when they had planned their big move from Coral Gables, only interrupted by a two-year stop-off in Palm Beach for graduate school for Lillian. Graduation sent them straight to Saint Augustine, where Joshua had accepted a teaching position at Flagler College. She loved natural sunlight and knew the benefits to mental health. Counting on their high privacy fence to do its job, sliding glass doors were covered with only thin, white linen drapes, so even when closed, they did not offer complete blockage, allowing warm sunlight to shine through. On cooler days, when bugs were absent, they left the doors open and enjoyed watching the curtains dance in the breeze. Leo would playfully bark and roll as they moved against him during his comings and goings to the backyard. He appeared to prance like a lion cub, confidently enjoying his domain as the lizard hunter and protector.

Light and sink fixtures, cabinetry hardware, and the staircase railing shared matching dark oil-rubbed bronze, a beautiful contrast to the white cupboards, furniture, crown molding, and wood paneling in most rooms. The two-story, three-bedroom, three-bathroom nest was much too big for just the two of them and their fur baby. Lillian ran upstairs to change her shirt again, this one wet with sweat from her afternoon walk. She stopped in front of one of the spare bedrooms, unclaimed and unused. The door had been opened by Joshua. It was an unspoken game they played. He opened it and she closed it. They were negotiating growing their family one day. He opened the door to remind her. She shut the door to clarify "not yet." Lillian's reticence over motherhood and her own conflicting speculation about her ability to be a successful parent brought her tremendous anxiety. So, she typically avoided the subject and redirected the conversation every time the subject came up. Joshua tried to be patient, but she could tell that her continued avoidance was testing his restraint.

Lillian remembered their last argument with a queasy stomach and rapid heart rate. They had enjoyed dinner outside in the romantic courtyard at O.C. Whites, where live music flowed, then a stroll around town afterwards to digest. There seemed to be an unusual number of children tagging along with their families that night. The walk home, after seeing the seventeenth stroller, started the drama.

"Why won't you talk to me about this?" Joshua insisted as he sat on the other side of the bathroom door, the sound of his forehead gently bumping against the wood and coming to rest as his hands probably pressed against the hard surface. She imagined his sheer willpower trying to melt right through. Lillian had locked herself in because she needed a moment to breathe after the heavy talk about having children that had ensued on the way home.

"You knew when you married me, Joshua, that I was damaged. I can't have children!" she had barked back while sitting on the floor and leaning against the door. She was sure Leo had climbed into Joshua's lap; she heard his cry.

"You can't or you won't?" he questioned, but he already knew the answer. There was nothing physically preventing her from childbearing.

"Won't," she said, affirming what he already knew.

"I want a daughter with your green eyes and blonde hair, Lil. I want a son with my brown eyes and brown, sandy hair. Or, you know what? Reverse that. I don't care who looks like who, I just want to make a family with you!" he desperately explained. Lillian had wept as she turned her emerald wedding ring, which matched her eyes, around and around her finger.

She stood paralyzed in front of the spare bedroom door, lost in the emotional storm that had been one of their biggest and most ongoing confrontations. Then her resolution returned, and she shut the spare bedroom door with a secure thump and walked back downstairs with her focus back on Leo.

"You just had a treat at the store. You are going to get fat, boy, then your back will suffer because your legs are so short!" she explained as she let Leo lead her to his cupboard, anticipating his after-walk treat. Lillian could not resist, rationalizing that the treat was healthy and organic. She threw the treat towards the hearth of the fireplace and sat down next to him as he devoured his chicken-flavored delight. Leo, already positioned on his pillow mat and savoring more time with Mommy, nestled in while she ran her fingers through his strawberry-blonde fur. Her fireplace took her back too. She remembered her client Sadie and the description of her childhood memories that began around her own family's fireplace.

Chapter 26

Sadie had grown up in a broken home. The physical structure of the house was strong and steady, and the mortar and brick were secure. The two-story house protected her family from several cold and harsh winters and hot, arduous summers that were the hallmark of the ever-changing weather of the Midwest. Even the raccoon family, who found shelter in the chimney, was not planning on moving out anytime soon. The family respected their masked inhabitants and never lit a match in the fireplace. It became a decoration on the south wall of the living room, a dark grotto, empty of the wood it should hold, echoing with noise of the hustle and bustle provided by the nocturnal busybodies.

"Tell me more about your earliest memories. Your bedroom, describe it to me," Lillian had encouraged Sadie, seeing value in knowing Sadie's childhood perspective. She had known that her source of pain started somewhere in her younger years, in her bedroom, but she needed more pieces of the puzzle to identify where the focus of therapy needed to go. Sadie described her yellow-and-white wallpaper, shaggy cream carpet, and overstuffed toy chest. Despite the stability of the structure, the house hadn't been prepared enough for the disaster that blew in from the far east in the mid-1970s. No blueprint, construction code, or extra installation could have prevented the devastation heading its way.

Sadie's father had served fifteen months in Vietnam. The traumatic experiences of the war spared her father's limbs and life but stole his mind and confused his emotions. Upon his return from the war-torn jungle, he had slept for days, quiet and hollow. Other times he had been overcome with sleeplessness, grief, and paranoia. The rooms that had once echoed with celebrations and laughter were displaced with mourning and outbursts of rage. Sadie's parents had divorced when she was only four years old. Her tender young life was rocked by a storm, leaving a painful aftermath that lasted years into her adulthood and brought her to Lillian's practice.

The description Sadie had given of her house prompted Lillian to engage her in a technique she called "home." Lillian, after grabbing paper and crayons that would normally seem inappropriate for an adult client, sat next to Sadie on the couch, a non-verbal gesture meant to communicate *I'm coming into your space; you can trust me.* Often, play techniques and art activities were the very things needed for an adult client to heal their inner child. Lillian began to draw a house, as similar as possible to the one Sadie had described.

"This house represents you, Sadie. Your trauma is all over your driveway, up the front walk, seeping through doorways and into the foyer," she explained gently and softly. She drew different shapes, including capital Ts to represent major trauma and lowercase ts to represent minor trauma, all over to represent Sadie's experiences that appeared to engulf the crevices of the house and its surroundings. "You can't get away from it. You also cannot place it at the curb. It will not be driven away by the garbage company. It will always be a part of you. What we have to do is sort through it, process it, learn from it, and pick a special place for it," Lillian had said, drawing a circle around an attic window and a basement window. Basements were a unique characteristic of a Midwest house not found in a southern house, due to ocean elevation. "See, here, it will always be a part of you, part of your story, but you won't be tripping over it. It will remind you of where you've been, what you've survived, but it won't define who you are, unless you want it to," she explained.

Chapter 27

L illian had engaged Sadie in EMDR. The acronym stood for Eye Movement Desensitization and Reprocessing, an evidence-based therapeutic technique used to remove or at least lessen the strong, emotional, negative feelings associated with trauma memories. Negative sensations frozen in time could begin to be resolved and healed. Essentially, changing the way past experiences were stored. It had been during her fourth session of following Lillian's index and middle finger back and forth, stimulating both sides of her brain, that Sadie had remembered a devastating night. She had suppressed the incident, but it had a lot to do with her self-identity.

Initially, she had recalled that her earliest memories were ear pain. She would lie on her parent's bed and whimper from the constant throbbing, which led to needing tubes and the removal of her adenoids. However, the quiet, consistent safety and EMDR treatment from Lillian had given Sadie the release of her earliest suppressed traumatic memory.

"I was four years old. My father was in a psychiatric hospital again and my mom had started dating. Her boyfriend was watching me so she could go out with friends. I was wearing my favorite pajamas, with feet and a zipper from groin to neck. You know, those northern pajamas that keep you warm and toasty? They were yellow, my favorite color. They matched my yellow wallpaper, bedspread, and bike. I called my bike my banana on wheels. Even my favorite food at the time was yellow. It was like sunshine surrounded me," she reported. She had also giggled, remembering the pleasant flashback. "I used to climb up on the kitchen table and eat the stick of butter hidden under the butter dish like it was a Snickers bar."

"Tell me more," Lillian had nodded and interjected as her fingers moved back and forth in front of Sadie's face.

"I'm sure I was sleeping. Maybe I was having a nightmare and calling out, but I don't think so. I remember wanting to be good. If I was sad or missed Mommy, I remember thinking, *Don't show it, don't let Mommy down.* He stormed into my room and yanked me out of my safe, warm bed aggressively. I felt scared. He dragged me out to the living room and stripped me naked. I began crying and shaking. I remember feeling cold initially, because I was naked, but fear must have warmed me up because I became sweaty. He made me put my hands against the coffee table in a position leaning forward. Now, looking at it as an adult, I see it as a position of humiliation and submission. He spanked me so hard and forceful in an upward gesture so that his hand and fingers reached my vagina too, sending pain sensations I had never known before. I peed and pooped all over myself. He told me, 'This is your fault, you little shit. Don't you dare tell your mother; clean this up!' I had to pick up pieces of my feces and flush it. I did my best to soak up the urine in the carpet. I mean, I was only four. I'm sure he cleaned up behind me because the next day when I came out, all evidence was gone. Like it had never happened. And that's how it had been treated," Sadie continued as she gulped back tears. Lillian had encouraged her to tell her more and had given her permission to cry.

"That monster became my stepfather, and I kept his secret my whole life. It wasn't until years later that I found out that he had been doing drugs back then. That actually makes it feel worse for me—the fact that I was left in the care of someone abusing drugs and not in his right mind. I had given myself a bath, the best a four-year-old can. I remember running the water and it had gotten too hot. I burned my toes, so I turned it cold and cleaned my bottom. I was freezing then. I put my pajamas back on. I cried myself to sleep that night, quietly, whimpering into my pillow." She exhaled.

Lillian remembered how Sadie had explained it was never something she had talked about until their session. What had emerged was an awkward and emotionally detached relationship—another father figure who had let her down and ruined her ability to understand the love of an earthly man. It had also twisted her understanding of a loving God, Lillian had realized. That understanding had gotten buried in Sadie's subconscious while her failed biological father relationship consumed her consciousness. Together, they had become a complex trauma that worked in tandem, inviting demons of shame, self-doubt, unworthiness, and the inability to love and be loved in a healthy way.

Sadie had spent weekends with her father when he was released from the mental hospital. There had been second and third hospital admissions interrupting the visits, but after those, her weekend visits were more consistent. The shock treatment her father received only suppressed his pain and nightmares; they had offered no cure for the trauma he had endured. The doctors could only push antipsychotics for his bemused mind. Sadie admitted that it had appeared to break her mother's heart to let her go on visitations, initially. As she had gotten a little older, her mother told her that she had kept herself busy, cleaning and organizing—anything to take her mind off her eldest child being in the hands of a man she once loved but didn't recognize any more. She explained that her heart slowed down on Sundays, anticipating Sadie's return—or possible failure to return.

"The irony," Sadie related to Lillian, "was that I felt safer with the man I left with than the man I lived with. My mom always seemed to be so relieved when she greeted me at the door. I could visibly see her face relax and she would smother me with this awkward, restricting hug. It happened every time."

Chapter 28

Sadie's father seemed to Lillian to have been a kind man with a pure heart. Time had established a relationship between father and daughter that had been full of shopping, movies, eating out, and shallow small talk. He had clearly loved her the best he could—she was all he had left, but he was unable to show her in the way she had needed. His love seemed to be communicated through materialism. He bought her clothes, toys, and junk food instead of speaking words and showing affection, the two ingredients Lillian knew most little girls needed to feel secure. In elementary school, Sadie had often written her name in school as "Sad," dropping the i and e. The teacher and her mother would correct it and she would add on the two vowels to please them.

"But that's how I feel, that's what my name should be, 'Sad,'" Sadie had whispered to herself.

As Sadie had grown older, the things she had needed from her father changed and became more complicated. She needed him to be strong and capable, give her sound advice and guide her into adulthood. However, he was barely able to make the simplest day-to-day choices of what to wear and what to eat, let alone understand the needs of an emotional and growing young woman. His ability to reason, articulate, and problem-solve had been left on that tangled, bloody, jungle battlefield with the souls of the men he could not save, despite his medic training and physical strength. All those men had been left behind, while her dad's life went on. He had been sent back to live a life he no longer knew how to live. He had reentered a society that did not understand or support the war, only offering judgment and ridicule.

His daughter had never understood what that did to him—the guilt and heartache he carried, and why it, along with the medications, had cut him off emotionally from relationships, from the entire world. The Haldol resulted in Tardive Dyskinesia, causing involuntary grimacing and facial changes that had scared her as a young child. In her eyes, it had transformed her father from a man to a beast out of a dark fairy tale. She figured out how to fix it with just a gentle whisper.

"Daddy?" she would ask. That had caused his face to return to normal.

"Yes?" had always been his quiet reply. Even if he wanted to, he couldn't have given her what she needed. It was no longer in him. It had been stolen by the Viet Cong and lay scattered and forgotten among the ashes of his fellow American soldiers.

Sadie had ventured out into adulthood, college, and career. Finally, she had been free of the home her mother had established a new family in, with the man who Sadie had a dark secret with. Although she had loved her younger siblings, she had never felt she fit in. She had felt protective of them and poured into their lives without reciprocation—the age gap was too large. She had intentionally kept the insidious detail about their father from them, to spare them. She had even kept it from her own mother, out of loyalty, always thinking about their feelings above her own. Lillian didn't miss the irony that Sadie was the first child in the family but had felt like an outsider. Frequently, that result seemed to be the curse in blended families—one that Lillian saw much too often, especially in blended families with hidden abuse.

Becoming emotionally detached and excelling in business had numbed the pain of the deep void within Sadie's heart; dealing with numbers more than people became her sanity. Numbers were safe, comfortable, and honest. 2 + 2 =4. No questions asked. No hidden agenda. No eggshells to walk on, and nothing to read between the lines.

Chapter 29

S adie had followed her college boyfriend to North Florida, completed a master's degree in finance, and embarked on a marriage way too young. She had never looked back. Once settled, she had moved her father across the country to an apartment near her; after all, she was all he had. Her marriage had ended in divorce within a year. He met someone else and left her. She didn't even care to fight for it. It was what she seemed to deserve. She stayed away from marriage commitment after that—she had a fear of failure, convinced that it was not meant for her, something that could never be. To her, love was an intangible concept that would surely crumble if she tried to grab ahold of it; case in point, she was divorced now.

She and her damaged dad had shared weekly dinners, movie nights, and errand runs. Eventually, he moved in with her for several years. Then, because of diminished memory and a few seriously unsafe choices—like turning on the oven without placing food in it and leaving the room or sleepwalking out the front door—she transitioned him to a veterans assisted living facility.

Sadie threw herself into achieving higher degrees and finding worldly success, thinking if she accomplished more and more, maybe then her father would be able to love her how she thought she needed to be loved. Lillian knew that Sadie still felt incomplete on the inside. That's why she had sought out therapy. She was still missing the validation little girls typically received from their father. The missing piece for Sadie was that crucial element that gave a woman a healthy sense of who she was, set expectations of how she should expect to be treated by a man, and the confidence that comes from being *Daddy's little girl.*

Not surprisingly, Lillian thought, she had occasional affairs with older men who were like surrogate father figures to her. They were safe because they did not want a commitment, just a few nights of pleasure.

Sadie had resigned herself to the belief that her life would never be any different. Convinced that her role as a daughter was to maintain the status quo, get what she could get from her father, initiate a hug here and there, tell him she loved him, and listen as he answered back, she plodded on.

"I love you, too," he'd reply in his automatic response mode. She could not hear or feel the love in his words. She took them as empty alphabet letters bouncing out of his voice box, lost and free-falling, trying to come together to create meaning, but always falling short, disintegrating in the air.

Successful and established Sadie, alone in a chaotic world full of people, found no comfort in the large amount of money in her bank account. She was unable to buy the identity she felt she had been cheated out of with her experiences with her father. When she came to Lillian, Sadie's silent screams of loneliness tormented her soul and echoed within the vacuous chamber of her heart. She was barely getting through meetings, and a power breakfast with her client one morning was a disaster. As she explained interest rates and investment risks, she became monumentally distracted. Weary from her personal angst, which was dredged up from her recent therapy sessions, she had headed out for a walk to clear her head. Meandering aimlessly down the hard cement on the city sidewalk, she finally turned back to her office, deciding to end her day shortly before lunch, eager to start her weekend early.

Sadie passed a beautiful, historic church tucked away between two modern office buildings in downtown Jacksonville, almost hidden and forgotten, yet to her, somehow standing out. Looking up at it, she felt its pull like a beacon of hope, a lighthouse that guides weary travelers through the dense fog of life, if only they would notice and receive its aid.

Chapter 30

O n that random Friday, in the late morning, the building clearly marked as a church had looked bigger and brighter than usual to Sadie. Something unseen had pulled her up the stairs, where she dropped, exhausted, into an empty pew. Her heart, fragile and broken, was finally ready to let go and cry out to the God she had learned about at Sunday school when she was a child. Her mother had made church her own sanctuary, an edifice holding groups of people, seemingly filled with peace despite the tragedies life threw at them. Her mother had been looking for hope in a marriage that ended up hopeless, and now Sadie, decades later, was looking for hope in a life she could barely hold on to anymore. She tried to remember how to pray to the God her Sunday school teacher had once called Father.

"Dear Father God," she whispered, her head slightly bowed and one eye open. Was He really listening? Was He there right now hearing her? She had not been in touch with Him for so long. She stared at the enormous cross hanging on the wall. She cried out to God quietly at first, the volume of her voice slowly raising as a wave of emotions washed over her. She fell to her knees, humbled and desperate, pleading with the Creator of heaven and earth for answers.

"Dear Father God, why? Why did you give me a father who can't love me the way I need to be loved? Why did You place him in a jungle that would strip him of his ability to feel and show affection? How could you stand by and watch a little girl, me, an only child, hurting and feeling incomplete? And now, a grown woman, how do I learn to love a man when no example has been set? How do I know who I am when my parents have never told me? What kind of God are you? You briefly entered my life when I was a child and vanished, for years. I remember that day when you touched my heart in Sunday school. I felt you there with me. My insides felt warm, and I felt safe. Safe from my father's illness, safe from the divorce, safe from my mother's pain, but then You were gone," Sadie raged, crying, hurting, and calling out to God. He was the God she knew of in her mind, but she never took the chance to know Him in her heart. He was the God she longed to get answers from and have a relationship with but was never shown how. Sadie didn't notice a pastor, who had silently entered the sanctuary from a hallway behind her, overhearing her lamentation.

Lillian had stopped Sadie to ask if she'd gotten a reply from God that day. Her own curiosity replaced her therapist instinct in an urge to know the answer.

"Did God reply?"

"Yes, He replied!" Sadie had responded. "Not like the God from the Old Testament who spoke out loud to His chosen people, not through a burning bush like Moses, or in a gentle whisper, like Elijah, but through an innate knowledge that has been with me ever since then! He connected the pieces of a puzzle I had collected throughout a lifetime, and they finally came together in that despairing moment."

Sadie tried to describe how God's Spirit spoke deep within her heart, in the quiet of her meditation, not because the stone building with stained glass held any answers, but because it took a complete brokenness and surrender in the stillness that she found within the walls to reveal the Truth, the answers tucked deep within her soul.

My beautiful child, my delicate and hurting daughter, I'm here; I've been here all along. That day your mother's boyfriend pulled you from sleep, stripped you, and beat you against the coffee table, I was there, grieving for you. The day you ran out into traffic when you were five years old to retrieve the basketball, I was there, steering the car away from you. The time your body burned with fever, at age eight, when your mother lay over you, begging Me to help, I drew that heat from your body and restored you to health. I wrapped my arms around you upon your graduation and sat with you in the stillness of your living room during the long nights of graduate studies. I was there waiting for you to invite me into your marriage, but the invitation never came. I was there when you drove across the state to visit a friend and you stopped at the side of the road. Remember when you took in the beautiful sight of My creation in the vast and colorful meadow? Remember the breeze that blew through you and you felt a touch of peace? That was Me, my daughter. I am with you always. I've been waiting for you to acknowledge me. I understand. I feel your pain and I love you. I grieve when you hurt; I hold every tear you have shed in my hands. The father I gave you, the earthly father who lost himself in that violent war, the earthly father made of flesh and bone, who survived and came home, an empty shell...he was never meant to fulfill all of your needs. I created you.

Lost in her private moment in the church, a voice in front of her had startled Sadie for a moment. "I'm sorry; I don't mean to overstep. I couldn't help but overhear. If I may? I feel a nudging to tell you something," the pastor stated as he approached Sadie. He sat down in the pew in front of her and turned his body toward her. "Perhaps God knew the kind of father you would need, who would bring you closer to Him. He knew that this pain you would feel, this emptiness you would experience in your heart, would draw you closer to Him. He waits. He is the only perfect Father. Only He can fill the void in your heart. How do you know who you are? Because He has told you! You are the daughter of the King; you are His daughter. Your earthly father does not define who you are, He does. He is everything; surrender to Him, completely. He fills the hopeless with hope. He will never let you down. He loves you unconditionally. No higher education, no man, no earthly accomplishments will ever make Him love you more than He does right now or when He created you. Give Him your life; let Him wrap His arms around you, feel His warmth. Let Him teach you about love and marriage and family through His perfect Word. Let go of your expectations of your earthly father. He has given you all he can. Let God complete you; let Father God fill the part of your heart that has been empty for so long. Get to know Him, take His love, and allow His healing. This is all God wants, more than anything else, it is to have a relationship with you, through His Son. Then with His strength, you will go and reach out to others who are going through the struggles that you have known. Reach out to those who are not loved by their earthly fathers in the way they need to be and tell them about Abba. You are His daughter, the daughter of the Perfect Father."

Chapter 31

S adie became focused with a new perspective. She made her way to the steps of the altar, too often used as a stage, where she prayed with the pastor for clarity. After a few minutes, he left her to her own thoughts and exited just as quickly and gracefully as he had appeared. Consumed in brokenness and peace, all at once, she fell to her knees upon the carpet.

As she slumped, she was struck by the familiarity of the color of the carpet—the same as the tile in the room at the mental hospital. It was the place she would go to spend time with her shell of a father, the place she knew too well and resented to the point of making her stomach churn. The flashback caused her to fall deeper into the carpet, on that platform, on that Friday, grasping what she could in her clenched hands. There she received God's affirmation. She quit running, striving, hiding, and avoiding.

She closed her eyes and imagined being back in that room filled with disappointment, as a little girl. She laid her cheek onto the floor and welcomed the soft feel. In her mind's eye, she saw her father sitting in the corner of the visitor's room, staring off beyond her face, beyond the pictures she drew him. Sadie took herself back to that moment in time and envisioned a third person. She placed Jesus there. His holiness and majesty too overwhelming to grasp, she wanted to place Him above her, a holy presence of comfort, but he came down from the ceiling, sat in the chair next to her father, and gently placed her on his lap. His smell was sweet, intoxicating! It was Jesus, the perfect Man and tangible God who held her hand and marveled at her colorful landscapes; he validated her artwork. He hugged her and told her how beautiful she was. Her earthly father, present physically, was still a non-participant in the memory.

That moment of conjuring up her unpleasant past helped her understand her pain for the first time. Sadie began to see images of her life like a PowerPoint presentation, snapshots of pain in which both her fathers failed her, and she placed her Father God there instead. Again, He appeared in the image of Jesus, the Son, fully involved and touchable. Even her memory of being taken from her bed at age four, stripped naked, and beaten until her bowels gave way, forcing her to have to clean herself up and keep the secret, she put Jesus there. He grieved when she was violated. He was there when she gave herself a bath and cradled her as she cried herself to sleep.

That day in the church began a process of healing that Sadie pointed out to Lillian. "Yes, but it was healing available to you all along, Sadie. You just weren't willing to accept it until you realized how the world continued to leave you empty and failed you again and again." Sadie had nodded to Lillian and then continued.

"I must have been dreaming," were the first words that she had said when she woke back up in the church. She had been disappointed; it had felt so real.

"Don't underestimate the work of God through dreams. You may have fallen asleep, but God never sleeps," the pastor had commented as he walked back through and gently reminded her.

Sadie had sat there thinking, finally realizing that she had been so determined to find her identity and happiness on her own, independent and capable, that she had missed the point! She had thought those were positive attributes. She had thought they made her a better person, that she had risen above her broken home and succeeded in a career. She was able to realize they only prevented her from completeness. Only through dependence on her Heavenly Father could her heart be completely fulfilled. Only through submission to Him and His Fatherly love, and the realization that He'd been there all along, her whole life, could she be the daughter she always longed to be, the daughter of the perfect Father.

"Oh, my Father God," she had declared right there on the church floor, "I've wasted so much time feeling cheated and unloved." Sadie prayed out loud, not caring who might hear or what they might think. "Forgive me, love me, show me your mercy!" she implored. "Help me let go of my resentment and anger, help me love my father for who he is and help me get to know You; show me how to know You. I've longed for You for so long but didn't really know what I was longing for until now." Minutes had passed, but it could have been hours or days. Sadie did not care; she had lost track of time. Finally, she left that building filled with a hope that things would be different. She remembered that she had learned two main ways God revealed Himself: through the Bible and through nature. She promised to tune back into both, and also, maybe a third way: people. She had known exactly what she needed to do then, and she knew precisely where she needed to go.

Chapter 32

Sadie had stood outside the VA nursing home after her encounter with God at the church, hesitant to enter, but eager to make things right. A gentle but flat smile greeted Sadie. A sense of loneliness flooded out of her father's room and hit her like a crashing wave.

"Hi, Sadie," he said. "This is a surprise." She had bound through the door, squeezing her father's neck, holding on with a passion that she never allowed herself to show before.

"Hi, Dad. I've missed you. I wanted to come and see you and tell you how much I love you, how much I've always loved you," Sadie forcefully whispered into her father's ear, out of breath and earnest. She reached in her oversized purse and pulled out a warm chunk of tin foil. She had insisted she make him his favorite meal, so she stopped at home and created two fried bologna and tomato sandwiches with mayonnaise, and chips added on for a crunch. Usually in a hurry, she made the first of many changes and decided to sit down and join him. She had enjoyed every bite.

Sadie forgave her stepfather as well. However, he would never admit to the abuse. In fact, he would call her a liar, compounding trauma upon trauma for an abuse survivor who is not believed. She would take control of what she could and never see him again. She had released him inside her heart and learned that her forgiveness toward him did not excuse what he did, but it set her free, and that was all the closure she needed. He was a hurting, broken man who hurt and broke a child. A hurt and broken woman she would be no more.

The most amazing thing about Sadie's transformation was the fact that nothing ever changed in her biological father. Sadie's sessions with Lillian revealed sources of pain and steered her towards an expression of her thoughts, feelings, regrets, and fears. Lillian urged Sadie to write journal entries of her painful memories and discuss them in session. She pointed out themes and asked open-ended questions to heighten Sadie's awareness of self.

In the months that followed, Sadie's relationship with her father, empty of regret and frustration, was filled with happiness and peace but not because of anything her earthly father did differently. He remained unchanged, emotionless, forgetful, distant; it was Sadie's heart, through the love of her Father God, that changed. It was Sadie who let her earthly father off the hook, accepted him for who he was, and let God fill the void. Sadie, who used to drop the "i" and "e" in her name in elementary school, embraced the Hebrew translation of her full name, Sadie: "mercy."

"God's mercy saved me!" she reported in her last session. Lillian had made sure to support Sadie with her open body language and words of affirmation. Lillian never heard from Sadie again until a wedding invitation arrived in the mail nearly one year later.

"Good for you, Sadie! You found love," Lillian declared with a smile when she opened it. She spoke aloud as she lingered by the mailbox. She did not go to the wedding, of course; it was a conflict of interest. She felt it was best to wish her well from afar and entertain thoughts of her wedding in the quiet of her mind. Lillian placed the invitation in Sadie's folder, alphabetized inside her locked file cabinet. She would keep it as part of her records for the next five years per law, seven years in all.

Chapter 33

Lillian recognized her reminiscing about past clients, stories of redemption and closure, as continued stall tactics and told Leo he was a bad influence.

"I could sit here and rub your belly all night, buddy, but Mommy has to go. Daddy will be home late tonight. I'll see you in a few days," she explained as she walked down the hall to use the bathroom. Uninvited, but accompanying nevertheless, Leo observed, as always, watching her every move.

"You're a bit intrusive, you know?" she laughed and added, "Of course, we watch you use the bathroom, don't we, boy? Fair is fair."

As Lillian used the last of the toilet paper, Leo anticipated their game and gave a bark, wagging his tail. He loved to fetch the toilet paper roll when it reached its end. Lillian squeezed it to give it some weight and did her best to throw it out of the bathroom and into the hallway. He darted after his target and pounced when he reached it. He brought it back quickly to continue the game of fetch. She lingered. Lillian affirmed him, scratched his chin, and continued with a few more throws as she cleaned and refilled his water bowl. She added a scoop of dog food to his food dish and then placed him on his dog bed. She knew he would not stay there but tucked him in anyway, feeling good that she did her duty as his mom. She knew he would untuck himself and run to the top of the couch, watching her through the window while she backed the car out of the driveway. She only glanced once, quickly; it was too hard to watch, as her heart ached to have to leave him alone.

The drive south, always easy and exciting in the past, was grueling. At one point, Lillian imagined turning the car around at the next available median rest area on the highway. She could run back into Joshua's arms with his promises that he could make it better, whatever it was. Why did she feel she was past the point of no return? Why did she feel her car was on autopilot and she was on a self-proclaimed path of destruction? *Because you are, Lil. This is your destiny,* confirmed her critical inner dialogue.

Chapter 34

D riving south, with palm trees lining her route, she found some comfort in knowing the ocean was off to her left, even though she couldn't see it. Lillian had more flashbacks, waves of memories of the August she was sent to stay with her aunt and uncle who lived in a unique neighborhood in New Jersey. They had a lagoon that had weaved through the backyards of properties before heading out to sea. It was the summer before her first year of high school, the summer of blossoming and first kisses, the summer of self-awareness and independent thinking, but it ended in a funeral and her father sending her away to his brother's home so he could figure things out.

Her mother's funeral was south of the bridge in Royal Oak, her hometown. Their church family offered emotional support, casserole dishes, and took care of all the arrangements. Enormous flower centerpieces lined the room. Lillian did not like flowers displayed at funerals. They were picked, so they were actually dying. After you mourned the loss of your loved one, then you watched the flowers die, a reminder of death for several days after the burial—she did not like that tradition one bit. She remembered it had been that way for her maternal great-grandfather's funeral also. He had hung himself from the attic rafters one summer during her elementary years, an unexpected plot twist for a young girl that had her walking past falling flower petals in the living room all summer long. She would quickly pick them up and throw them away so her mother and grandmother wouldn't feel sad if they saw them. Lillian mourned for her inner child. She still didn't understand how the tangible grief of that loss hadn't been enough to make her mother fight to live. Her mother had experienced the pain of a suicide and then willingly passed that pain directly to her own daughter a few years later. It made no sense to her. Even now as an adult, as a therapist, she couldn't comprehend her mother's selfishness. Was it more like an unstoppable cycle, something her mother hadn't been able to control? Then would she also succumb to it herself? Was it a family curse?

She held her breath, waiting for Jeremiah to show up and pay his respects, avoiding distant relatives as best she could, hearing over and over how sorry everyone was and giving awkward hugs and kisses that offered no comfort to her. Dean and his family could not afford the long journey but sent a card and floral wreath to show their love and offer condolences. Dean called Lillian multiple times at home and sent multiple letters in the mail. She only replied to one weeks later when she was finally settled down in Florida with her dad. She scribbled on a postcard that caught her eye at a gas station, a giant pink flamingo surrounded by palm trees.

> *Thank you for caring. Thank you for your kindness and your kisses. We moved away. I probably won't ever see you again. I pray you have wonderful high-school adventures and find love. Lil.*

Chapter 35

When Jeremiah finally walked into the funeral home, Lillian burst into tears. She was convinced he was the only person who could comfort her, the only person she wanted to be comforted by. She ran towards him. He kissed her forehead and wrapped his arms around her. He cupped the back of her head in his right hand and steadied her with his left arm around the small of her back. For a moment, Lillian imagined him confessing his feelings for her, holding her close and admitting he truly loved her. To her, he was her lover who returned from war and would never let her go again. They would go to their bed chamber this night and conceive a child in a fit of desperate passion.

But instead, he said, "I'm sorry, Lil. I'm so sorry."

In anguish, she blurted out, "My father is sending me away to New Jersey and then moving us to South Florida. Please take me back up north with you. Don't let him send me away, Jeremiah, please. I love you. In four years, I will be eighteen and we can be together. Please, I can't lose you too." She leaned forward and made a deliberate plea in his ear. Jeremiah, taken back, let go of Lillian and pulled her into a hallway out of the main viewing area.

"Hey, Lillian. Shhhhh, sh, sh. I love you too, you know that, but like a brother, not like a husband. That would be so wrong, my sweet little friend," he explained. Lillian fell to her knees while grasping his suit coat and cried louder. She would not accept his response.

"Please don't say that. You love me how I love you; I know you do!" she pleaded. Jeremiah faltered. He inhaled deeply and then groaned, joining her on the floor.

"I love you like a brother loves a sister or a best friend loves a best friend. I cherish you like one of the most important people in my life and I would travel oceans or climb mountains to rescue you if you called out. That does not include romance, Lil. That is different. Love does not always equal romance. You should know that I have wrestled with feelings of love and appropriateness the past two summers. My grandfather has been my guide and he reminded me how important timing is, how critical it is to honor the trust of a blossoming heart. You are still so young. And so vulnerable. You will find the one who can give you all those things, when the time is right. You're wounded, hurting, and need time to grow," Jeremiah clarified as he reached into the inner pocket of his suit coat and retrieved a jewelry pouch. "I had this bracelet made for you. When you wear it, remember God has a plan for your life and you are loved." He took her left arm and attached the bracelet. She loved him more for that, knowing she was right-handed and would prefer a bracelet on her left. It had a cross etched in it, a simple symbol that represented so much that she didn't fully understand. Underneath, a Bible verse location was carved: 1 Peter 5:10.

"Look up this verse when you get a chance. You are God's beloved, Lil. Wear this to remember who and Whose you are," Jeremiah added. He stuck around for the day, remained close during the ceremony and burial. She could see the pain in his eyes. She could see the wheels turning in his mind. He was wrestling with something.

"You are special. You are loved. Keep looking up." Jeremiah tried to speak to her soul back at her house that evening. He shook Lillian's father's hand and pulled Lillian aside one more time. His embrace felt all-consuming, as if it was the last one he would ever give; and as it turned out, it was. Jeremiah's eyes filled with tears when he walked away from her, down the front stoop. His pace quickened. Lillian thought it was probably because her sobs were too painful for him. She shouldn't have cried so loud. She must have scared him away.

Many years later, she had heard through the grapevine, that his grandfather had died shortly after. He sold the property and used the money to relocate south of the bridge. He did indeed quit engineering and completed medical school. Lillian had silently celebrated. He married a fellow doctor and had four children; his oldest daughter was named Lillian. She had beamed. He deserved every blessing in his life, in her opinion, for the kindness and appropriateness he had poured on her and for the godly seeds he had planted.

"I will get the house on the market, pack it up, get things settled in South Florida, then fly you down. We have a rental waiting for us and when this house sells, we can use the money to buy our own down there." Her father repeated the plan that night after the burial. She felt dismissed. She let her feelings be known that evening when he hung up the phone, after making all the arrangements and emerging from his home office.

"So, Mom's suicide wasn't a wakeup call, Dad? Now you're going to send me away. Let me go back up north. Let me stay with Jeremiah. He has always taken good care of me; he loves me, and I love him. I feel safe with him. Let me go be with him!" Lillian commanded, finding the volume knob for her voice.

"This is not up for discussion or debate, Lil. I am your father; you belong with me. You're a child and Jeremiah is a man. We are going to South Florida to start new and that's final," her father responded, looking as though he had been sucker-punched. Lillian refused to go unless she could bring Benji with her. He had become more protective since her mother's death, with an intuitive sense of her anger and sorrow. She insisted and agreed to pay the extra money for his fee to fly back with her. Her savings account held a mere seven hundred dollars from babysitting and birthday cash over the years. Her father relented and told her he would pay the fee, agreeing without discussion or another argument. Lillian was satisfied.

Chapter 36

For the first two weeks in New Jersey, Lillian had barely left the spare room. Her aunt and uncle encouraged her to run errands with them, get out of the house, and assured her that ice cream was on the list. Even though it was the Northeast, her aunt and uncle had the Southern warmth and charm brought with them from Mississippi. They were hospitable and accommodating unlike any other people she had ever met.

During previous visits, she would have already been sunburned, with water-clogged ears and sore muscles from countless dives to the bottom of the lagoon to check the crab cages. She would have already made several visits to the ocean's shore by now. Lillian considered going with her aunt and uncle. After all, coffee ice cream was her favorite and she had not had any since that day with Jeremiah when they played catch. However, she had changed her mind and opted out, asking if they'd bring some back for her. Not being pushy, they had agreed.

She laid in the guest bed with the window open, a warm breeze coming from the lagoon which led to the Atlantic Ocean. She wore a red tank top with matching lipstick that Shelly had given her when she left for the summer. Shelly had told her that now that she was a woman, she needed a woman's lipstick…no more tinted lips from berries. Her denim shorts revealed long, skinny legs kissed by the sun. Her long blonde hair, that would darken a shade or two but sustain highlights from the sun by the time she graduated high school, was pulled up in a messy ponytail. She could always think better when her hair was up. She fondled and rotated the bracelet Jeremiah gave her, thinking up ways she would find him and storm into his life when she was eighteen. She would kiss him in a way that would make him never want to let her go. She still had not looked up the Bible verse. She was purposely protesting "words breathed out by God through men" thousands of years ago.

The oscillating fan offered a few seconds of breeze before leaving and returning, hitting an open magazine, creating a crinkling paper tempo every thirty seconds. Next to her bed sat a warm glass of unfinished water. Her summer reading books were piled high. Her father had sent a box, priority shipping, with books; surely it was his attempt at keeping her busy and distracted. She usually enjoyed reading; she looked forward to the reading lists every year and would spend hours navigating the literary worlds of authors who could paint pictures with their words. Benji would lay between her legs, often opening one eye when she would turn a page or talk out loud to a character, ready to get up and follow with the slightest hint of her movement.

Her mind had been racing and she had been overwhelmed with reasons why her mother might possibly have chosen to leave her by taking her own life. She reached for Benji for reassurance, realizing for the first time that he wasn't there.

"Ben! Here boy!" Lillian called to him. She was sure he was attempting to find yet another way to get through the screen door and chase a bird or squirrel. Her stomach had started to churn as her heart began to race. Her search for him became more frantic. Lillian scanned the living room, checking his favorite spots, as she saw a piece of the screen door ripped in the bottom left corner. Benji was nowhere in sight. She had remained hopeful and continued calling his name.

Barefoot, she ran into the backyard, off the stone pathway she helped her uncle lay, much like the pathway she had helped her grandfather make outside the sauna, and onto the pebbles that covered the grassless yard. With pain shooting through her feet from the rocks, she continued looking around the corners of the house, her eyes following the fence line, avoiding the water initially, since she could not see him on the long dock. She kept trying to convince herself that there was no way he could be in the water, unless he slipped.

"There was no way he slipped," she whispered desperately. He had been outside with her countless times. Sure, he would run to the end of the dock and taunt the dog across the lagoon, barking at him from the adjacent dock, but he always stopped before reaching the edge. He listened when Lillian told him to settle down and leave the poor dog alone.

"Your territory ends at this dock. You don't have to defend against foreign lands, for crying out loud," she had explained. It was his protective and territorial instinct that always made Lillian feel safe when she was home alone or had just watched a scary movie and was a bit on edge. She knew no one was getting by Benji and that she was in safe paws.

"No, God, please no!" she pleaded through soft sobs and whispers. Having exhausted all other areas, she made her way to the dock and looked over. There ten feet below, floated Benji, lifeless. His long black-and-tan hair drenched and matted; he was floating on his side with green seaweed wrapped around his short legs. Lillian screamed. Bypassing the ladder that she had climbed down multiple times when she went for a swim or grabbed the crab cages for her uncle, she jumped directly into the lagoon and swam to Benji. Gulping water through sobs, she was a strong swimmer, but she struggled to stay afloat. Her shock and disbelief weighed her down heavily, like she was being pulled by a strong force from the bottom of the sea floor. She fought for her life and grabbed a handful of seaweed attached to Benji's legs, pulling him into her.

"No, no, no, no!" she gurgled when she realized she was too late and that he was gone. He was breathless. He was dead. Overwhelmed and exhausted, she managed to secure Benji under one arm in a football hold while climbing the ladder with the other. She went into a daze. How she managed to get to the top of the ladder and safely onto the dock was a mystery. She only remembered her aunt and uncle, once back with ice cream in hand, yelling from the house. They had run straight towards her as she sat drenched, sobbing, and holding her most precious treasure, her best friend. She pulled at pieces of seaweed, trying to get every single piece off of him, secretly hoping that life would re-emerge if only she could unveil him.

Chapter 37

*S*urely, now there is proof that God is a punishing God, she had thought. Her mother killed herself. Jeremiah abandoned her. She had been rude and argued with her father. She had protested the Word of God, and now God had allowed her best friend to drown.

"How much do I have to handle?" she whispered, deflated. The cycle of blame and negotiating began. If He were too busy, He could have sent an angel to block the end of the dock and force Benji to return safely to the house. She heard about angel armies being all around in the spiritual realm. Where was hers? Still reeling from her own mother's funeral, she prepared the cardboard box that had held the summer reading books and other clothes her father had shipped to her. With her aunt and uncle's permission to bury Benji under his favorite tree in their backyard near the dock, she prepared his coffin. He always looked so handsome in red, so she wrapped him in a red blanket.

Her mind flooded to his first Christmas party. She had worn a red-and-green checkered dress, and he had worn a matching sweater. She had printed the photo of them posing on the staircase, covered in red tinsel. Using popsicle sticks and ribbon, she had created a frame with a string for hanging as a tree decoration. Lillian had presented it to her parents as a gift on Christmas Eve. They had a short-lived tradition of putting on new pajamas after church and opening one gift before bed. She remembered opening her illustrated children's Bible with excitement when she still had the wonderment of God. She had shared her thoughts about Adam, the first man, who had the fun task of naming all the animals.

"I know Adam named a dog, 'dog,' because dog spelled backwards is god and God is loyal, loving, and never holds a grudge. He is our best friend, just like dogs are, so that makes sense to me," she had affirmed.

Her hands had trembled as she prepared Benji's box and gulped back the tears of now-painful affection she had shared with him over the years. "Please, honey, let me do it for you," her uncle had insisted. He wanted to dig the grave to spare her the additional pain.

"He's my loyal and loving best friend. I have to do this for him," she insisted back, through sobs. She took the shovel and dug a hole deep enough to fit the cardboard coffin in. Barely able to see through her tears, she used crayon to write his name, birthday, and death date, sat for a minute, and created a poem in her head. She wrote it down on the long side of the box. Her hands were shaking. Her heart was broken, but her mind was focused. She would complete her task.

> Best dog, best friend, with you gone, my heart will never mend. Run fast, run free, please don't ever forget me. I love you, good and loyal boy, Benji. XOXO, yours, Lil.

Her hands had stung from the rubbing of three new water blisters that formed from shoveling. They had popped quickly, the warm liquid dripping down her fingers and making her grasp difficult. However, she was stubborn and would finish what she started. While examining her hands, she suddenly noticed her bracelet missing.

"Oh no! It must have come off in the lagoon!" she had panicked again and insisted in a desperate whisper. The sun was going down. She had to hurry. Without a second thought, Lillian had run to the edge and dove back into the water. She swam hard to the bottom, desperately patting the sand to find the one of only two things she had left of Jeremiah. She held her breath so long, her lungs felt they would burst without oxygen. Crabs scattered as she disrupted their home. Placing her feet on the bottom, she pushed off the ocean floor, reaching the surface just in time with a loud gasp for air.

"Lil, what are you doing? Are you okay?" Her uncle had stood on the dock, looking down.

"I lost my bracelet. I can't find my bracelet. I need my bracelet! Jeremiah gave it to me. Please, I have to find it. I need my bracelet!" Through coughing and crying, Lillian had tried to explain. Without hesitation, her uncle jumped into the water and pulled her towards the ladder.

"Come on, honey. Climb back up there and let me go down and look," he asserted. After quickly retrieving a mask and snorkel, Uncle Kenney had searched with what little daylight they had left, without success. He had promised her he would go back down the next day at first light and do his best.

Lillian placed the last of the dirt over Benji's grave, repositioned rocks over the dirt, and walked into the house like the walking dead. Her Aunt Clara met her with a warm towel and a soft hug.

"I'm so sorry, sweet girl. Do you need anything, honey?" she inquired with the soft, sweet voice of an angel—if one had ever existed, she'd thought. Lillian had only managed a shake of her head. There were no words. Once in her bedroom, she had stripped off her wet clothes, naked and vulnerable, only enough energy to put on Jeremiah's Michigan Tech sweatshirt she had stolen out of his bedroom—now the last thing of him left. She had sprayed it with his cologne her last day in the north. Then she fell into bed. She held a spare pillow tightly, pretending she was in Jeremiah's arms and that he would never let her go. She slept deep for two days, only getting up once to use the bathroom and to take a sip of cold water that Aunt Clara must have left by her bedside.

Chapter 38

I can't open my heart anymore just to feel the pain of loss over and over. God is mean and wants too much. The concept had swirled around in her head for years. Lillian had been sure she would never love again. She would never have another pet. She would never get close to anything that she could lose. But here she was, nineteen years since that summer when she made that proclamation over her life. She had a passion to heal hurting people, a loving, devoted husband, and a dachshund always in tow offering cuddles and kisses. Maybe she was not a lost cause.

Time did not heal all wounds, though. She would never try to sell that to a client. Time just helped you figure out how to live with the pain and get comfortably uncomfortable with a new normal, a little more wounded, a little less trusting. Open wounds would eventually seal, leaving a scar and a story. Maybe there was not a demon behind every bush and maybe she should not live her life waiting for the rug to always be pulled out from underneath her. But there were demons, and rugs did get pulled out.

Tears welling in her eyes from her fragile memory, Lillian chided herself to get out of her head and turned on the radio. She was unsure why these heavy memories of her own past and specific clients' pasts were suddenly and nearly unrelentingly flooding her mind. As she drove into an environmental storm, she recognized that she was revisiting old wounds and in doing so, opening a new one. Her brain hurt and she felt nauseous. She grabbed for some crackers and took a drink of the ginger ale she'd bought at the gas station.

Chapter 39

The radio announced updates on Hurricane Mateo, a category 2. It was slowly passing over the Bahamas at 12 miles per hour, with wind gusts of up to 98 mph. Gaining strength, it was still on track to hit South Florida as a Category 3 or 4, late Friday night or early Saturday morning. She remembered the category 5 that had hit South Florida directly, during the first semester of her sophomore year of high school. She and her father were hunkered down in the hallway closet as multiple tornados ripped through Coral Gables and its neighboring area of Kendall. The worst hit was Cutler Ridge and its neighboring city of Homestead, sitting to the south.

Homestead was flattened like an atomic bomb had been dropped, causing insurmountable destruction, many deaths, and homelessness. Families moved away and never came back. Lillian's school and her father's church did multiple fundraisers to offer relief. It was always in the act of helping others that Lillian felt the most fulfilled. You could always find someone with greater pain than your own.

She swerved slightly. A turtle was slowly and steadily crossing, bringing her back to the moment.

"Ahh! Faster, little one. Faster!" she encouraged the turtle, relieved that she navigated around without incident. Traffic was heavy northbound as coastal residents evacuated, allowing Lillian to have an almost open road to herself. She could smell the thick humidity in the air, allowing it to invade and consume her car through the open sunroof. The police sirens headed north.

"No doubt someone was texting or answering an email while driving," she mumbled. The red and blue lights reminded Lillian of an unexpected but welcomed friendship with Elijah Blake and his wife, Hailey. Hailey was a decade older than Lillian, and Elijah almost a decade older than Hailey.

Elijah was the depiction of a man after God's own heart, just like her own husband Joshua. He was devoted to love, family, and peace at all costs. But he didn't start out that way. Elijah had a history of objectifying women. He grew up in the church and loved God but did not truly understand what having a personal relationship through Jesus Christ meant. He didn't know how to take the idea of church and apply it to living. Until he fell in love with Hailey. He objectified her at first too, but when they sought God's heart together, his mind and heart transformed.

Hailey was a psychotherapist, just like Lillian, but she specialized in family dynamics and addictions. Specifically, she ran a group for survivors of loved ones who died of drug overdose. Her favorite focus was group work, where Lillian preferred individual sessions and offering trainings in a teaching setting.

Lillian had provided the local police department a training on trauma and handed out her business cards several years back. Elijah introduced himself.

"Thank you for that great trauma training. You really should meet my wife—she is a licensed therapist too," he offered. The two couples went to dinner at the Crown and Bull on St. George Street one Friday night and an unbreakable bond was formed in the quaint British restaurant.

Later, Lillian would come to learn that Elijah wrestled his own demons regularly. He saw too much evil to not have to fight with a few here and there. Although he knew they couldn't possess him because he was filled with the Holy Spirit, he knew they could try to attach to him, attack, confuse, lie, and manipulate. It was usually at night when the world went silent that they appeared. He would do his best to not wake Hailey. She was too in-tune not to notice; she wrestled demons too. Often the antidote would be a roll over into her arms. They would overcome the darkness with passionate lovemaking, fueled by an intense sexual chemistry. Every hug hello and goodbye looked like they knew it could be their last embrace. Their love was deep and noticeable. Elijah and Hailey knew spiritual warfare and they had lived to tell about it.

Chapter 40

Elijah loved military history and had a great sense of humor. He was the calm in life's storms. He was the guy who walked into a room and you just knew everything was going to be okay. He had broad shoulders and a defined physical strength. His black hair was peppered with natural touches of white. He was always "packing." Even when off duty, he wore a gun around his ankle or in his belt, hidden under his shirt, ready for a terrorist or criminal to make a move. He was ready to sacrifice his life on or off duty to save lives around him, without hesitation. He sat with his back to a corner, always with an eye on all exits. This was not a negotiable option. All who went out to eat with Elijah knew the seating arrangement. It was the status quo, no questions asked.

Elijah brought humor and lightness, but little emotion. Emotion to a police officer was like a chink in the armor. It was becoming emotionless that saved many cops from the corrupt chaos they had to reign in everyday. It was the warped sense of humor that protected them from feeling the pain that came from desperate radio calls. The multiple incidents of battered spouses, abused children, addicts, fatal car accidents, and a sense of hopelessness was a heavy load to carry during their twelve-hour shifts, in addition to a bulletproof vest and gun belt. It was usually the detour to the bar that got them home a few hours later and helped them sleep and suppress the haunting memories. All so they could wake up and endure another shift. Elijah struggled with wanting to get straight home to his family, while still decompressing with his colleagues with a nightcap. It was a delicate balance juggling loyalty to both worlds.

Hailey was an expert in family dynamics because her family of origin was complicated. Hailey and Elijah always said that God brought them together so they could fight the good fight of breaking the unhealthy family chains. They both had cycles that they had to break to start a new, God-loving generation. They clung to the teachings in Matthew 10 and Luke 12, where Jesus declared that he came to divide family members—those who chose to serve the Lord and those who chose to serve themselves. Both sides of their family persecuted them for jumping off the dysfunctional, worldly train. They had ridden that "crazy train" for many years, though, thinking they had to stay on it.

Elijah's family included an overbearing mother who overstepped boundaries and kept a wedge between him and his brother, who was ten years older than him. Elijah's mother's greatest talent was probing her sons with questions, taking pieces of the information gained, going to the other son, and slandering each one to the other. The intent was to keep herself relevant, stirring the pot of dissention, and to be needed as the information holder and giver. When her daughters-in-law entered the picture, her tangled web became more complex, layered, and convoluted. She would put herself in the middle of each marriage, slandering each spouse to the other, back and forth, daughter-in-law against daughter-in-law, husband against wife, brother against brother. When grandchildren were born, she would show favoritism to one over the others and undermine the parents. She created an environment of chaos and paranoia. Family dinners and holidays got more uncomfortable with each year. The lies and half-truths spawned by Elijah's mother alienated the family members from each other and caused the group to shrink smaller and smaller each year. Eventually, Elijah and Hailey's family circle was comprised of only them and their four children. So, they started their own traditions.

Before Elijah met Hailey, he had had a brief marriage with a woman who spun her own webs, just like his mother. She lied about being on birth control while they were dating, and they conceived a son. Elijah had married her to be the provider and do what he thought was the right thing. His faith in God grew during that time. He clung to God's promises and began to look at things through spiritual eyes. His wife wanted nothing to do with God and made it clear that Elijah had been her pawn, for a baby. Then the taunting became toxic. She threw insults at him and dared him to hit her, hoping he would, so he would lose his job and go to jail. It was hell on earth and God rescued him. Unequally yoked and with no peace in their home, they separated and divorced. The divorce had cost him twenty-five thousand dollars and almost two years of his life. Lawyer tactics, stalling, and legal fees, they were the final games his wife would play to try and hurt him, but they had backfired on her. The court saw him more stable and fit to be the custodial parent, and she had to pay him child support.

"Can't you just stay with her for your son and cheat on her if you're unhappy?" His mother had once again placed herself in the middle and provided her unsolicited, uninspiring maternal words void of wisdom.

Chapter 41

Hailey's family was blended. Hailey was the only child between her parents, who had divorced when she was a toddler. Her stepfather had abused her, in a similar way to Sadie's, and then married her mother. They had three children of their own. Hailey was parentified at age eight. She could change diapers, sort laundry, and clean up an entire Thanksgiving dinner like no other child or adult by the age of ten. She had learned how to survive among two broken homes, people-pleasing, mute and living below the radar. She could read people and know when to keep her mouth shut, when to start doing chores to keep her caregivers happy, and when to get lost to avoid a confrontation.

Hailey's stepfather set an example of gossip and insulting family members, devaluing other people's lives. Hailey later realized it all as an attempt to keep the focus off his own underlying issues, his demons. Her most vivid memories were car rides to Thanksgiving dinners, dance recitals, or Christmas holidays when he would belittle or make fun of the people they were visiting. Then, they would enter their doorway, their world, with smiles on their faces. He had been two-faced, double-minded, and manipulative, and Hailey had detested it. He stood *with* everyone and everything, therefore stood for nothing. He was a chameleon, a bandwagon jumper, a fence straddler who would jump over to the side of whomever he was with while working behind the scenes to serve himself. Others' lives, including Hailey's, became open territory to ridicule, dissect, or persecute.

Her stepfather's fifteen-year affair with another woman, throughout his thirty-year marriage, warranted his perpetual deception, lies, schemes, and toxicity in the family unit. She did not consider him a bonus parent; he did not step it up and provide security. He lost an opportunity to fill a void in Hailey's life, one left by her own biological father—not present a lot and then deceased. He had been a career soldier, a well-decorated helicopter pilot for the U.S. Army killed tragically in a training exercise.

Her stepfather had been the perfect example of how the sins of the father can destroy a family dynamic. Using Hailey and Elijah to babysit his children, he carried on with his secret relationship.

Was it Hailey's destiny to hide her abuse as a toddler only later to be used to hide his love affair, while a wife and mother navigating her own family? She had finally stood up for herself when she worked through her trauma and learned assertiveness in graduate school.

"Why couldn't you keep your wife's mouth shut?" his last words had been to Elijah, when truths were revealed. It had taken all of Elijah's training as a police officer not to knock him out. First, for what he had done to Hailey when she was an innocent toddler, and second, for involving them in his marital drama, and, lastly, for his deception in destroying what should have been a loving, blended family. Eventually, Hailey had lost relationships with her siblings too. Their loyalty to him surpassed their loyalty to her.

But Elijah and Hailey had found each other, fallen in love, and raised his son as their own. However, the combination of a meddling mother-in-law and bitter ex-wife was destructive for their son. Instead of a celebration of love and unity, it was a cycle of division and competition. He lived among two worlds: love, law, and order versus materialism, lawlessness, and drugs.

It started with marijuana, which led to oxycontin, which led to heroin, and then the heroin laced with fentanyl that had eventually led to his death. Both sides of the family judged their tough love and boundaries, of course. Not one of them had ever entered the thick of it with them and not one person ever asked them their truth. Both sides of the family and an ex-wife, who Elijah and Hailey had to cut ties with, all became best friends through social media. They made themselves seem like heroes, like they were superior, and enabled their son. Their divisiveness only contributed to his end.

Elijah and Hailey had learned to be okay with that. God knew their truth, and that was all that mattered.

They started an organization in his name, for families battling the drug world, to offer support and resources. Their peace and hope came from the knowledge that their son had accepted Jesus as his Lord and Savior as a child, prior to his addictions. He had lived in the promises of God for years before yielding to the darkness of drugs. They both believed he was in the presence of God, no longer lost, but found and welcomed home. One day, they knew they would see him again. Hailey had not attended the funeral and she accepted that she would be judged for that too.

"Funerals are for the living," she had said. "There wasn't one living person there who I felt safe mourning with, except Elijah, who did attend. But we already had spent years mourning together with our other children, for the son and brother the drugs were stealing from us. My bonus son's physical death was just an extension of that grief. No one was honest about how he died. I stayed away from the charade. No more battles for me!" She had shared her feelings with Lillian when they met up for an early morning run one day. Lillian offered her arm a squeeze as she felt Hailey picking up the pace with a burst of energy. She understood Hailey's feelings about the funeral and the importance of feeling safe with people you mourn with. She had been there herself. She thought about the dishonestly surrounding her own mother's death. She saw a strength in Hailey she wished she had herself.

"I was there when he was seven years old, and he accepted Jesus as his Lord and Savior. No one can take that from me. That's all that matters. Our son, *my son*, lost his way, but didn't lose his salvation," Hailey added through heavy breathing.

Chapter 42

Hailey had studied and understood the insanity of blended family dynamics unlike any other therapist Lillian knew and unlike any textbook she'd read in graduate school. Depending on the age of the child or children and the emotional maturity of the biological parents, *when* bonus parents entered the scene determined how the stage was set. Often, the younger the child or children, the more accepting they were of having a healthy attachment to their bonus parent, especially if they became their primary caregiver. However, the anger and residual pain held by the biological parents frequently caused bitterness, toxicity, and alienation between the child and the bonus parent. Lillian had seen relationships that could and should be beautiful and secure for a child become forbidden through emotional sabotage, negative seed-planting, and manipulation.

She was quick to warn her families about the balance of teaching children responsibilities but not parentifying the oldest sibling and giving them roles with too much adult authority. Hatred and resentment for the parent and the oldest siblings could ensue if roles were blurred and lines crossed. Older children of blended families often had a harder time accepting a new parent and would hold resentment, anger, or bitterness. It caused stressful dynamics, not only between the child and parents, but in the marital relationship as well.

"Maybe that's why God cautions against divorce, if it's possible," Hailey shared with Lillian one night, sitting at an intimate corner table on the second floor of the Columbia Restaurant on St. George Street. They had been sharing the 1905 salad and a carafe of red sangria. Elijah and Joshua were at the bar across the room, engaged in their own conversation as they tasted a new whiskey. Lillian noticed that Elijah maneuvered himself at the bar's end, near the kitchen door, with the ability to see the entire room and all exits—predictable. They were safe. She smiled and turned back to Hailey.

"Not because divorce and remarriage are supposed to be evil, but because He knew the pain and suffering blended families could create and have to endure. Look at King David's complicated and destructive family dynamics we see throughout the Old Testament, and he was a man after God's own heart! Look at what Joseph's half-brothers did to him out of jealousy, believing he was favored by their father and deserved death!" she added with a sigh. "I fainted at my mother and stepfather's wedding, during their vows, when I was seven. I've always wondered if my subconscious was shouting, 'Mom! No! He hurt me. You're next!' I split my chin wide open. Blood was everywhere. My cousin, who is a doctor, took me to a room off the church sanctuary and gave me a butterfly bandage. I think my body had a reaction to the reality of a lifetime with my abuser. I lived an entire childhood and early adulthood wearing a mask to please that man, keeping him happy so he wouldn't hurt me again." Hailey lifted her head up towards the ceiling and used her pointer finger to trace the skin under her chin, revealing a thin scar, only noticeable if she pointed it out. Hailey had become the biggest advocate for blended families because in her heart, her own had failed.

"Stay married! But if you can't have peace in your home, if you're not equally yoked, and you decide to go separate ways, embrace as much love for your children as possible!" Hailey stressed. "Even Jesus was given an earthly father to fill a role in his life." She had created homemade signs that hung in her therapy office: *Blended families can and should be a beautiful thing.* Another sign hung under it: *Leave your children out of your drama.* And one more: *Bonus parents are your child's chance at extra love.*

Hailey explained why she painfully cut ties with her family. "I grew up feeling emotionally and mentally unsafe and suffocated in my family. And, honestly, just exhausted. The secret of my abuse was a ticking time bomb inside of me. When I finally spoke my truth, I wasn't believed or validated. I put up a wall to protect myself and walked away. It has taken me years to sort through all of those layers of my life. And as I get closer to God, I realize that, sometimes, you just have to get out of people's way, so God can work." Her statement gave Lillian pause. She nodded her head, knowing all too well through her trauma lens the lasting negative effects of hidden childhood trauma.

"You are so brave, Hailey," she validated. Instantly, her mind shifted to Jeremiah getting out of her way and it struck her that he may have done it in love, so God could work. *He must have known that he needed to let me go. I was young and confused, and perhaps he got out of the way so God could work in my life. As long as I was consumed with thoughts about him, I would not fully surrender to the Father. I still haven't surrendered to the Father. I have no idea how to do this,* Lillian thought.

"I forgive my stepfather. I hope he finds peace in his life." Hailey went on, "I had hoped that over time my siblings could acknowledge my perspective and be back in my inner circle of trust, but it's proven that it has always kept us vulnerable to the enemy's schemes. I pray their hearts soften so they can know God and maybe we can reunite one day safely. I want them to experience God's love and peace more than anything. I want to be together in Heaven. It just doesn't seem like it will be through me." Lillian nodded in understanding as she reached for more sangria.

"People say blood is thicker than water, but people in God's family who are covered by the blood of Jesus have the thickest and most powerful blood of all because it has washed away all of their sins and binds them to the Father. God can and will fill family roles for those who have lost loved ones or whose loved ones turned against them because of Jesus," Hailey rationalized passionately. Lillian thought about Jesus' twelve disciples leaving their families and jobs to follow him. They became their own brotherhood. Even at the cross, Jesus saw the sorrow in his mother's eyes and told her and John that they would be mother and son moving forward. Hailey and Elijah had become the sister and brother Lillian and Joshua never had; Lillian and Joshua had become the siblings that Hailey and Elijah lost.

"When a family member is cruel or speaks lies over you, when absurdity ensues all around you, yes, sometimes it's just sinful human nature.

But when the attacks don't make sense, I think it's strategic and intentional spiritual warfare. Satan uses lies to divide and conquer families. He delights in it! If you don't believe the gospel that tells you God is for you, that God is for His children, the insanity demons will try to suck you in. You will be filled with confusion, anxiety, frustration, and anguish. You must acknowledge, claim, and believe that God is for you. Step back, breathe, and know the angels are all around you with swords drawn. When things don't make sense, God is battling darkness on your behalf; you need only be still." Hailey completed her diatribe with tears in her eyes. Lillian's eyes swelled with tears as she grabbed Hailey's hand under the table.

"I love you, sister; you're safe with me. You know I'm for you, right?" Lillian emphasized through blurry eyes.

"I love you too, sister. Ditto to all that!" Hailey gently laughed through a wet snort. Lillian joined in the laughter just as Elijah and Joshua made their way back.

"The testosterone is back. Bad timing? Should we…?" Elijah swooped down and kissed Hailey on the cheek, tasting the saltiness of his wife's tears. He squeezed her shoulder. Lillian eventually learned that it was a gesture that said, "I see you. I'm with you. I got you."

"No, it's perfect timing; the estrogen wants you back right here," Hailey cut Elijah off and replied while patting her right palm over her heart.

"May I propose a toast?" Hailey asked as she lifted her glass with her right hand. Elijah grabbed her left hand and squeezed, awaiting his wife's proclamation with a smile that could cancel all fear. Lillian and Joshua grabbed their glasses and followed suit.

"May we be the great patriarchs and matriarchs of our families! May our children and children's children know the sacrifices we made so they can know the love and sacrifice of Jesus. May no man or demon ever break our family bonds," Hailey proclaimed. They clanked glasses and drank. The proclamation of future children caused an unsettling wave of emotion inside Lillian as Joshua squeezed her hand and looked at her with desperation.

Chapter 43

A few months previously, Hailey had asked Lillian if she would facilitate one of her group therapy sessions one week. She was headed to
Key West with Elijah to celebrate their anniversary.

"This group. It's heavy and dark, Lil, but I still think you would be
great. It consists of all relatives of addicts who died by drug overdose. They
each blame themselves in some way or another," she warned Lillian. Lillian
reminded her friend that she preferred individual and family work but
reluctantly agreed to put on her "group hat" to help Hailey out. Hailey was
grateful. "Remember, let them run the group. If they follow the group rules,
which are listed in the room, let them keep the flow going. You are just
there to redirect and validate as needed."

"Even though it is not my favorite cup of tea, I *did* enjoy my group
work during internship. I got this," Lillian affirmed.

On her way to group that one night, she was reminded of Hailey's
perspective on drugs and addictions. Lillian knew too well the insanity
of addictions from her internship work, but Hailey was the expert, and
she had firsthand experience. Drugs seek to first destroy everything that
is good in and around the user and then make their final move—to kill.
Those with a drug addiction will lie, steal, and cheat, all while justifying
their actions. Within families, they will divide and conquer. If there is any
unsettled business between family members, the addict will seek it out and
use it, causing a division, a rift, a disintegration of relationships.

Chapter 44

It is dark and heavy, Lillian processed in her mind. Hailey was not being overly dramatic. The group welcomed Lillian. They agreed that if she was a colleague of Hailey's, then she was alright by them. Immediately, it began. A woman in her fifties started.

"I had an abortion because my boyfriend didn't want our baby. I quickly hooked up with someone else and used him to get pregnant. Then I ended up losing custody of our child by the time he was two because I was selfish and prideful. I spent two decades belittling and essentially bullying my ex and his new wife. I tried poisoning my son against them during visitations. I hated their love and peace. Their family grew and I couldn't get pregnant again no matter how hard I tried with my new husband. He eventually left me for my best friend. My life was chaos, and my son died of heroin overdose. So, I got rid of a child, lost a child to drugs, and can never have another child. My womb is sealed, and I have no siblings. My bloodline will cease to exist when I die. I'm all alone now." She had a haunted stare as she shared the painful details of her life. Next was a woman in her late thirties.

"My oldest sister had a different father. She was like a mother to me, very loving and giving. But when she started her own family and actually became a mother, I was unbelievably self-absorbed. She had started therapy because she needed to work on some unspoken childhood trauma. She confided in me and told me that my father abused her when she was a toddler. I was so angry, I told her she was a 'whore' and a 'liar' and that I hated her. I sent her a text. The last thing I said to her was that she was a sociopath who deserved to die alone. I texted her oldest daughter and tried to turn her against her own mother for no reason, other than my own rage.

My sister overdosed in a hotel room within twenty-four hours of my text. So, I get to live with that. To make things worse, my father admitted on his deathbed to abusing her. Now they're both gone." Lillian reflected on the power the tongue has to give or take life. Then a man in his early thirties took his turn.

"My sister's kid was a rebellious daughter. I lived with my sister for some time when I was getting on my feet, after trouble with the law. She and her husband opened their home to me with loving arms. I was struggling with my own identity. I could see the choices their daughter was making and could see them show compassion but set boundaries. I mean, I was only there nine months; I had no right to have an opinion or make a judgment. I was just thankful they took me in. She was getting 'high,' breaking curfew, lying, and becoming aggressive. Her behaviors were affecting the younger children in the home, so she went to live with her grandmother for a while. They gave her an ultimatum. 'You can come home if you take a drug test and see a therapist with us.' She refused. She died a few years later. I never even asked them if they were okay throughout the whole time. Their daughter would slander them and contact me for money to pay her bills, and I would send it to her. Now, I realize, I was probably helping her pay for her drugs. So, she's gone, and I have no relationship with my sister and her family anymore. I should have helped them reconcile, not taken a side." Lillian internally processed the mistakes made when judging a situation from one perspective, especially that of an addict.

The stories kept going around the room. Dark and heavy, dark and heavy. Lillian's heart hurt for these people. Her inner dialogue began. *Hailey does this weekly? How is she going to move these people forward? How would they find peace and hope?* When Hailey returned from her trip, with pink cheeks and a rejuvenated spirit, they met for iced coffee and sat on the sea wall overlooking the bayfront, filled with sailboats. She processed the group session with her. Hailey listened to Lillian's feedback and shared her own thoughts.

"They will only find peace if they surrender to Jesus, girl; you and I know that. They may spend a lifetime with their guilt, shame, and regret weighing them down. Satan churns all the evil in the world, but like I said before, I think he is most fond of being in the center of breaking up families. He wants to keep us separated from God first, but then he wants to destroy earthly families because there is strength in numbers, and he wants us weak. The group is a sounding board, but their freedom comes in laying all that dark heaviness at the foot of the cross. Freedom in Christ." Lillian didn't comment, but inwardly she questioned Hailey's assertions.

Chapter 45

Normally, excitement would emerge when Lillian drove on the highway through downtown Miami. The city skyscrapers were signs of the final leg of her destination to Coral Gables. She would roll down all the windows, despite the temperature, and turn on the local radio station, blasting the music of the city. This time, the windows stayed up and the music was off. She shut her sunroof.

She passed the exit to the Miami Hospital on her right, where she had enjoyed her undergraduate internship. She spent hours interviewing postpartum mothers and collecting data for her psychology professor's longitudinal study. Not far from there was the Dade County Jail, where she exchanged candy bars for urine samples from newly incarcerated male inmates with drug histories for her criminology professor's research project. Both had been challenging assignments that grew her confidence in talking to people like her—imperfect people with messy lives. She learned how to conduct structured interviews and demonstrate empathy.

Blended Hispanic and Caribbean Island cultures, rich with exciting music and delicious food, had awaited her and Joshua on endless past trips. Sometimes, they'd stop to indulge before they checked into their hotel. Their favorite restaurant to eat at was Versailles, on Southwest 8th Street, in the heart of the Cuban community. They started with yuca croquettes. Then, Joshua always ordered the chicharrons, while Lillian ordered the roast pork Cuban style. They shared off each other's plates while washing their meals down with Cuban mojitos. Café Cubano for dessert gave them the caffeine they needed to enjoy time together late into the night, not wanting to miss an ounce of the energetic nightlife.

Driving past her alma mater, Lillian reflected on her undergraduate studies where she had met Joshua, who was a graduate student at that time. She had declared a major in psychology and a minor in sociology, with a focus on criminology. She discovered courses of study that grabbed her attention and challenged her intellect. She felt comfortable learning about the darkness of man's mind, especially because she had experienced it first-hand, too many times, by the age of adulthood.

After the big move across the country just a few weeks before high school, Lillian fell in love with the heat and ocean South Florida had to offer. She decided to stay for college and was content trading the fresh lake waters of her youth for the salt waters of the Atlantic Ocean. She never returned to Michigan and her childhood lakefront summer adventures after the death of her mother. The humidity of the Southern city offered the familiarity of the sauna from her youth. It was comforting to walk to class on beautiful brick pathways outlining ponds and palm trees while sweat pooled on her upper lip and lower back. Once again, the thick air, making it difficult to breathe, reminded her that she was alive.

With a heavy burden of grief that caused consistent depression throughout high school, Lillian pushed forward. If she didn't keep moving, the quiet and the stillness reminded her about her mother's pain medication and her grandfather's old rope hanging from attic rafters. *Her destiny too?* She was able to uphold superb grades and be an award-winning member of the softball team as the first-string catcher and co-captain, all while singularly carrying the weight of her mother's death, the loss of her dog, the loss of her Northern childhood best friends, and the loss of Jeremiah. Add in the complications of a forbidden love affair or two, an abortion, betrayal, and guilt, and it was no wonder that she began college with a new, consistent dance with anxiety. The anxiety butterflies that she had been able to release and outrun throughout childhood summers, and which were dormant during the depression years, roared back with a vengeance.

Chapter 46

Beginning in the winter of her junior year of high school, Lillian was preparing for softball season. They had the talent to make it to the playoffs and battle for the state championship. She often had played catch with the baseball players on her off time. It reminded her of playing catch with Jeremiah after they met.

"Don't take it easy on me. Go all out. Treat me like one of the boys, please," she would remind them. Switching between baseballs and softballs kept her on her toes. She would laugh that as a catcher in full gear, behind the plate, mask on, mask off, an umpire breathing on the back of her neck and invading her personal boundaries, she would be a dirty hot mess by the end of her games. Her teammates had perfect ponytails, unsmudged mascara, and intact lip gloss.

They had an unblemished season and then won their final game, making them one of the top two teams in the league, but it ended in tragedy for Lillian. She would not play for the championship; she would not play another game. In fact, she would choose to never play catch again.

During the final inning, they led the opposition by three runs. There were two outs; all they had to do was hold them and get one more out. Bases were loaded and the hitter aimed at a hole in left field. Runners were on the move and Lillian knew it was coming down to a tag-out by her at home plate.

It happened exactly as she saw it. With two runs scored, the first-base runner was rounding third, with the hitter close behind her. She had to get the first runner, or they would tie it up and go into overtime. If she missed her and missed the hitter, they would lose. The throw came to her, out of reach and to her left, and she had to move her whole body quickly to receive it. That put her outside the baseline. Normally, a tag-out would be made with two hands. The glove hand would be holding the ball and the free one would be wrapped around to protect it and strengthen it. She could only reach the runner by diving back and stretching her gloved hand out alone, leaving it weak and vulnerable. She tagged her out and they won the game, but the consequence was a dislocated thumb inside her glove. The powerful runner had run through the thumb portion of her glove like a steam engine through fog.

Chapter 47

W hen it had happened, Lillian had pulled her arms into her chest, fell into the fetal position, and screamed. Her teammates who had begun yelling and celebrating ran over to smother her in hugs, but they realized she was not on the ground overwhelmed with joy. She was suffering in pain. They called for their coach.

"What hurts?" he had asked.

"My hand, my thumb!" Lillian had winced and replied. She could feel the adrenaline rushing through her body and began to imagine she was leaving her body just to escape the pain.

"Stay with me, Lillian, you're going to be just fine," he had reassured.

Not having a relative at the game because her father was leading a church function, the men's baseball coach stepped in.

"I got her. I'll take her to the hospital. I probably shouldn't, because it means I'm breaking rules, but we can't just wait around. It's what I'm going to do," he decided. He picked her up, just like Jeremiah had done. Lillian felt cradled and safe. In her mind, she was transported back to her grandparents' property in the north. Her coach told him not to, that he would call an ambulance. But the other coach had ignored him and placed her in his car.

"I'm so sorry, Lil. Hang in there. I'm going to take care of you," he promised while driving the short distance to the hospital.

He had called her father from the waiting room, helped her get her glove off, held the ice on her thumb, and answered as many questions as he could for the ER staff until Lillian's father showed up. He stayed until she was discharged, thumb relocated and wrapped in a temporary cast and sling.

The relocation of her thumb and ripped tendons had resulted in surgery weeks later and had kept Lillian out of commission for many months. Another rug was pulled out from underneath her. Mentally still a very innocent, damaged child, she had been unprepared to process additional trauma and extreme disappointment. In her adult mind, reflecting on that time, it did not surprise her that she ended up having an inappropriate sexual affair with the baseball coach that lasted until she graduated.

She had lost her virginity to him. He had rescued her, and she was able to play out the fantasies that had never come to fruition with Jeremiah. *He was single and thirty-five, why not?* she had reasoned. At seventeen, she had felt wise enough to consent, although, by law it was actually statutory rape. She was not eighteen, the age of consent in the state of Florida, and he was well beyond twenty-three years old. So, the Romeo and Juliet Law would not protect them, had they been found out.

They were never caught though. They became experts at keeping their secret. They lived in the shadows. The excitement of doing the forbidden was part of the thrill. However, she was ashamed and knew Jeremiah would have been disappointed, too, so she created another mask. Initially, she wore a mask of the content pastor's daughter for his congregation. She wore the mask of the obedient and independent child for her parents. Then she put on the mask of the strong daughter of the dead mother, who could bury her pain and be everything her friends and teachers expected her to be. During the affair, she wore the mask of the secret lover. She wondered if she stripped herself of all these masks, who was she really? Soon after her eighteenth birthday, right after her high-school graduation, he had broken it off with her.

"Best to go our own ways. Hey! I had fun though. You'll meet someone in college, and…blah blah blah," he had explained as he went on and on, but she had not heard what he was saying anymore. The rejection was a familiar, painful feeling that she shoved aside to cope.

A few months after that, she found herself in the arms of her youth pastor. After years of processing, writing psychology papers, and counseling others, she eventually came to see that in her youth, she did not know her value. Two significant men devalued her, creating a fractured sense of self. The self-destructive relationship patterns people play out with one another, tossing each other back and forth, lover to lover, were examples of humanistic, flesh-filled living. Sex was a gift, but when it was not monogamous, handled with care, the way God intended it, it often resulted in heartache, disease, unexpected pregnancies, and dreadful remorse.

Chapter 48

Anxiety in college, for Lillian, had presented itself with stomachaches and increased heart rates, especially when assignments were due. There were racing thoughts of what ifs, catastrophizing scenarios, and existential crises. She would think, *I had an abortion and God is sure to punish me.* Then, the unresolved grief from her mother's death, her dark road of unforgiveness for herself, the baseball coach, and her youth pastor all added to the anxiety. Initially, her coping mechanism was a mixture of productivity: *Lil, get your assignments done and you won't stress about them; make lists, cross things off.* And then there was her classic avoidance: *Lil, lay out on the beach and drink more until you don't care,* the angel and demon constantly battling on opposite shoulders. In fact, the demon won for most of her first semester, causing her to go on academic probation, with the risk of losing her academic scholarship and possibly getting kicked out. Lillian's father's pastor salary could not afford the credit hours at "The U," the nickname given to The University of Miami.

Then entered Joshua. The handsome, intelligent, dedicated graduate student who immediately loved Lillian unconditionally. He could have had anyone he wanted. Females and males drooled over him. He only saw Lil. He was helping Dr. Suarez grade papers in his religion class as a favor, because his graduate assistant was out of town for a family emergency. Lillian's tragic, painful words towards God in her paper, "What Spirituality Means to Me," penetrated his heart.

He had made an excuse to stick around when Dr. Suarez passed back the papers, putting hers on top to see who wrote it. He was blown away that not only was she beautiful on the inside, but she was beautiful on the outside, too. He pursued her. He made himself relevant in her world. He figured out her schedule, her dorm, her library habits. He offered more help to Dr. Suarez, often stepping on the toes of his graduate assistant when he returned. *You're being a little stalker-ish Joshua; be cool,* his inner dialogue would whisper. He eventually admitted all his schemes to Lillian early in their relationship.

Then he pursued a friendship with her. He was her saving grace. He saw her imbalance and her ugly burdens but embraced her brokenness and beauty. He was the son of two doctors who worked out of country, beyond the United States borders, for most of their careers. With him alongside them, off and on since he was a toddler, Joshua lived an atypical life—first hanging out of a baby sling, and then, once able to walk, working alongside his parents, Joshua was wise and experienced beyond his years. He had an unusual combination of book smarts and life experiences. He was charismatic and full of positive life energy. Not unexpectedly, people were drawn to his aura.

Joshua had flicked the demon off Lillian's shoulder repeatedly, without apparent exasperation. She was exasperated with herself enough, while he seemed to fill the space with comfort, hope, and patience. Even after she told him her dark, unforgiveable sins, he stayed. It was only their third date, when she had wanted to tell all her burdens to him so he could run before things got too serious. They had dinner at the on-campus restaurant, the Rathskellar, known to the coeds as "The Rat." Joshua knocked on her dorm room with a bouquet of yellow daisies, typically symbolic of happiness, joy, and friendship—and a giant smile. She was instantly physically attracted to him the first time she saw him. With each conversation, she was drawn to his mind and heart unlike any other, except Jeremiah. So, she did her best to scare him away, assuming he too was sure to leave her.

Throughout dinner, Lillian had been restless. After taking only three bites of her chicken sandwich and maybe two sips of her iced tea, Joshua grabbed her hand and led her on a walk around the giant lake in the middle of campus. That walk around the lake alone could be the perfect romantic date for those on meal plans and no extra spending money. He weaved his fingers through hers, holding her hand firmly, and raised her hand to his face. On the back of her hand, he dropped a light kiss.

"What's on your mind?" he had asked as he led her to sit down on a bench, positioning himself to look deep into her eyes. He turned towards her intentionally, easily maintaining eye contact. She unleashed her dark past.

Chapter 49

Expecting him to judge her and run away fast, he stunned her when he reached out and hugged her instead. He held her firmly with the solidness of his broad shoulders and told her he was sorry she went through it all. She had been speechless. Then Joshua took a deep breath and explained his perspective.

"There are no unforgiveable sins, Lil. All sin was paid for on the cross, and when you repent, you are as white as snow." Then he flipped the script on her even more. He insisted that her mother did not kill herself because Lillian was unlovable.

"Do you think she is burning in hell? Do you think I will see her again?" She shared a fear she had never spoken out loud. She echoed what she overheard a Catholic girl say in high school the year a classmate had taken his life.

"My priest said all suicides are sin and you burn in hell. So that sucks." Lillian did her best impersonation. Joshua shook his head.

"Let's look at this intellectually. If sin makes you burn in hell, then you, me, and that priest will be burning in hell together—we sin every day. That's the whole point of Jesus dying on the cross. Sin is sin. People can't pick and choose which sins allow you into Heaven and which sins keep you out. The point is Jesus; His death and resurrection cover all sins." He continued, "You told me that your mom knew Jesus, Lil. It sounds like her brain was tired from battling the depression, and sometimes the darkness is too much for the human condition to bear. If she accepted Jesus as her Savior, despite her choice to take her life, she is in His presence. No more pain, no more sadness. You will see her again." Lillian had gulped back tears as Joshua continued.

"You know why Christianity means so much to me and I know it's The Way? Besides the fact that it is rooted in history and evidence, other religions are based on doing something, living a legalistic life, obeying the law, saving yourself. Christ followers, who understand the message appropriately, live in love and forgiveness. Jesus did it all. We are new creations in Him. We don't have to do anything—just accept his sacrifice."

He continued to explain how wrong it was for the men, a baseball coach and youth pastor in positions of authority, to take advantage of her. They were at fault, they were wrong, and, according to Joshua, they would be held accountable by God.

"The truth will always reveal itself, Lil," he insisted. He explained how they saw her vulnerability and woundedness, using their status and skills of persuasion to justify fulfilling their sexual desires. He leaned in and said, "But if they repent, Lil, if they asked God for forgiveness, remember, they are forgiven, too." Lillian understood everything Joshua said to her with her intellect but was not ready to acknowledge it in her heart. And so, their love story had begun.

At the time, Lillian had thought about telling him about Jeremiah. He reminded her of him in so many ways, but better, because she was no longer an off-limits child. She was a woman. She decided that she would keep him to herself for now and she would treasure her childhood fantasies in her own secret, locked-away world until she was ready to speak them into existence. She thought if she verbalized them, they would begin to dissipate, be blown away, and she had not been ready to let Jeremiah go just yet. It was her memories of him alone that gave her hope and kept her moving forward.

Chapter 50

Joshua was Lillian's accountability partner for passing her academic probation period and keeping her scholarship. He brought Chinese food, pizza, and subs every chance he got to her dorm room. He would study with her, check her planner, help keep her focused and purpose driven. Some weekends were spent in Coconut Grove and Miami Beach after homework and studying were complete. When the weather permitted, Joshua would put the top down on his jeep and take her to Monty's Raw Bar at the marina, their favorite escape in the Grove. It was their go-to after spending a few hours on the beach, soaking up the Vitamin D and enjoying the melting pot of culture. When they didn't want to spend time looking for parking in the city, they went to the beach on Biscayne Bay, a little closer and a little less crowded.

After dinner, they enjoyed walking the romantic streets in Coconut Grove, popping in and out of boutiques, feeding ice cream to each other— chocolate fudge for Joshua and coffee for Lillian. The drive back to campus took them on roads winding through beautiful neighborhoods with early Bohemian influences, the smell of jasmine, and giant oak trees providing overhanging shade and mystery. They would take turns choosing a different house randomly each time they drove through and pretend to live there. The chooser would make up a story about the house, giving a description of the inside, how many children ran through the halls, and what kinds of careers they had pursued. Joshua always added children. Lillian entertained the idea of one dog.

When Lillian began developing stronger and unprecedented feelings for Joshua, her inclination to self-sabotage would resurface periodically.

She was still the girl with the distant pastor father, suicide-lost mother, drowned, darling dog, lost childhood friends, wasted virginity, tainted womb, and frustrating childhood. Most importantly, she was the girl who expected God to punish her every other minute of the day. She still didn't feel deserving of, or know how to accept or return, love. She routinely reminded herself that she would be the weight holding Joshua back from greatness. Everything about Joshua and his gentle, loving approach had felt so right, so she simply had to push it away.

Chapter 51

S till lost in her thoughts, Lillian remembered one pivotal evening. It was a typical muggy Friday evening. Joshua had purchased tickets to the on-campus musical of *South Pacific* at the Ring Theater. They had been looking forward to it for weeks because of their shared love of musicals. Lillian bought a fitted black dress with a subtle flair at the bottom, just above her knees, and black, open-toed high heels that revealed her candy-apple-red painted toenails. With red fingernails and lips to match, gold jewelry, and blown-out hair that magnified the sun's naturally streaked highlights, she was almost ready. She had dedicated extra time with her flat iron to make natural waves. When she looked in the mirror, for a moment, she had thought for the first time ever, *I look beautiful.* She looked away quickly, fearing she would see the predictable ugliness emerge if she stared too long.

She planned to walk with her roommate, Samantha, to frat row and then loop around to the theater, where Joshua would be waiting for her outside. He had offered to meet her at her dorm room and walk with them, but she insisted she would meet him there. She had also wanted some girl-time. Even though they lived together, it seemed that her and Sam barely talked, with two different schedules and social calendars. Plus, she wanted to make an entrance with her approach to him, hoping to hear a gasp when he saw her all cleaned up. In her mind, she would be walking in slow motion, with romantic instrumental music playing, like in a dramatic movie scene. He would stop in his tracks and say, *Wow! You look beautiful!* He'd clutch his heart. She would accept the compliment gracefully and own it.

The loud, welcoming music rolled out of the houses on fraternity row like a city block-long orchestra, beckoning college co-eds to partake in the excitement inside each house. They had stopped at Alpha Epsilon Pi, where Sam was meeting her boyfriend.

"Come inside for just a minute, Lil!" Sam begged. She hesitated, knowing she should stay on her path towards Joshua, but decided to humor her friend. That one decision changed the trajectory of the evening. Several Jell-O shots later, alcohol-vulnerable, having lost track of time and once again underestimating her own self-worth, she found herself in the arms of Chase. Chase was in several classes with Lillian and had his eyes on her all year, but everyone knew she was Joshua's girl. He had recognized that she was tipsy and alone, which excited him. And thus began the age-old game of the hunter versus prey.

"Hey, Lil, need some help?" Chase had asked with a smile as he maneuvered her against the wall, buried his head in her neck, and took a deep breath. "Your smell is intoxicating," he added. He told her how much more he could offer her than Joshua and moved towards her lips. Lillian remembered feeling dizzy. She closed her eyes and felt a rush of sensations as his lips crashed against hers, wet and warm. He dragged her, intoxicated, through a hallway into a vacant bedroom. Tossing her on the bed, he started to explore up her dress.

She opened her eyes, suddenly realizing it was not Joshua, and she pushed him off aggressively. He recovered quickly, steadied her, and went in for another taste. Immediate regret for her decision to enter the frat house that night overwhelmed her, and she desperately wished Joshua were there to rescue and protect her. *What was wrong with her? Why did she put herself in another vulnerable position with someone who did not value her?*

"Stop, Chase!" she managed through clenched teeth, determined to rescue herself this time. He ignored her command and pushed in harder with his hot breath on her neck. One hand groped her right breast while the other forced her to touch the hardness under his shorts.

"No, stop!" she said angrily as she managed to knee him hard. Within seconds, someone had yanked Chase off Lillian and he landed forcibly against the wall across the room, face first, with a loud thud that split his lip.

"She said to stop, predator. Don't ever touch her again," Joshua's steady and determined voice warned from behind him. Realizing who it was, Chase threw up his hands in a quick surrender and slithered away like the snake he was. Joshua fixed his shirt cuff and grabbed Lillian by the hand.

"Come on, sweetheart," he whispered as he helped her up and gently led her out to the sidewalk. Lillian began crying and apologizing. Joshua, angry, confused, and annoyed, but thankful he'd found her before something worse happened, *shhh-ed* her and had led her to his off-campus house just a few blocks away. As they walked in silence, his breathing returned to normal, and his temper began to soften. He realized he didn't mind eating the cost of the theater tickets if it meant finding Lillian and keeping her safe.

Chapter 52

Lillian stopped just before getting to his house. Pulling her hand from his, she stumbled forward and fell to the ground.

"Just leave me alone, Joshua. You're always there, saying the right thing, swooping in. Tra-la-la Joshua, life is perfect, God is great, everything is going to be okay! Just leave me alone," she slurred as she wretched all the alcohol-saturated Jell-O out of her stomach onto an undeserving bed of buttercups flourishing in the neighbor's front yard. Joshua ignored her protests and scooped her up, carrying her into his place.

"Yah, I guess I probably deserve that. But you're no prize at this moment either, so I'm not leaving you alone, little miss cranky pants," he insisted as he gently tucked her into his bed, gave her two aspirin, a piece of lightly slathered peanut butter toast, and a bottle of water with electrolytes.

"Do you have a peanut allergy?" he inquired before allowing her to inhale the snack. She shook her head no. He kissed her on the forehead, which triggered a memory of Jeremiah. Lillian reached toward him, ready to surrender her body and soul to him too, but he stopped her.

"You've been devalued enough. Yes, I want to make love to you, more than anything, but not like this, not like the two men before me. I have self-control and I will show you how love should be," he proclaimed.

"I'm sorry for what I said. Why are you so good to me?" Lillian whispered. Joshua had answered back, despite her already-closed eyes and her deepened breath; she heard everything he said.

"Because you have stolen my heart and will be my bride. I will spend my life loving you and protecting you. I will slay demons for you, Lillian

Michaelson." He took her hands and whispered a simple prayer of healing and protection over Lillian.

He slept on the couch, checking on her four times in the night. She pretended to sleep but felt his presence. It was apparent that they both slept lightly, listening intently to one another. He later confessed, on the evening that he proposed to her, that he had never felt that way about a woman. He said he couldn't explain how he knew that he wanted to spend the rest of his life with her. The thought of not having her in his life or being with someone else made him feel nauseous and sad. He had been determined to prove himself worthy to be her husband and to show her that she was worthy to be his bride. The Holy Spirit was in both, he decided, and chose to start there. Although he realized she appeared to be constantly running from God and always waiting for His wrath, he was determined to bring her back to the loving arms of the Father God, the Father God he knew.

Chapter 53

The next morning, Lillian awoke to the smell of coffee and bacon. She allowed her nose to guide her and greeted Joshua in the kitchen with a hug and yet another apology.

"I forgive you; stop apologizing," he insisted.

"This is your house? It's beautiful," Lillian commented as she scanned the room.

"Thank you, my parents gave it to me," Joshua replied.

"They gave you a house?" Lillian followed up, beyond curious. Joshua had hesitated over the bacon for a brief moment, then he opened up about a piece of his own past.

"The day I graduated with my bachelor's degree, we celebrated at Mai-Kai Restaurant and Polynesian Show. It was a great time! We drove separately so I could bring several friends. After a long and memorable evening, I hugged both my mom and dad. I planted a huge kiss on my mom's cheek. I am so thankful I did that. I couldn't understand how I'd beaten them home after dropping off all my friends. My phone calls kept going to voicemail. When the doorbell rang several hours later, my heart dropped into my stomach. I knew what the police officers had to tell me before they even opened their mouths. My parents had been killed by a drunk driver on their way back home." Joshua cleared his throat. He took a deep breath and forged on. "The money they left me paid off the house, my undergraduate debt, and is paying for my graduate degree. It also bought my jeep, and a few traveling adventures I escaped on during the early stages of my grief process. Thanks to them, I have no debt and a nice house I can sell one day to buy a place of my own free and clear." He paused. Staring down at the sizzling pan, his voice became barely a whisper. "I would trade it all. I would pay it back. I would pay their mortgage myself too...if it could just bring them back."

Lillian gasped at the cloudy memory she had of her insensitive comment to Joshua the night before, specifically her *Tra-la-la,* comment. She opened her mouth to apologize yet again, and Joshua stopped her by gently placing his finger on her lips.

"Hey, you didn't know. You're not the only one with dark clouds, you know. Yes, I have experienced incredible loss and grief. For a while, I wasn't even sure that it wouldn't break me. I'm not completely sure that in some way it actually didn't. But I ran to the Father for comfort. I needed to put some meaning into the situation and so I chose to honor my parents, by continuing my studies and doing the things I love. I know that it's what they would have wanted. I had to continually choose to embrace the good in the middle of the bad. Honestly, I still do. What you see that looks positive and joyful is a choice, Lil. That doesn't mean I always feel positive. Always feel joyful. Never feel broken. As far as I can see, that's just not how grief works. It doesn't just heal away. Healing feels more like holding the loss in just one hand so I can scoop up the joy with the other. I don't show the pain to just anybody. My grief is still very personal and private, but I have scars too."

Chapter 54

After that, they began running together, not only to burn off the food they enjoyed eating, but as a plan to increase her endorphins and decrease her anxiety. Joshua, already a consistent, strong runner, helped Lillian conquer the 4.1-mile campus perimeter loop quickly. She became addicted to running. She woke up and outran her demons every day, sometimes seven days per week. First mile, demon of guilt and his fraternal twin brother, shame. Second mile, demon of grief. Third mile, demon of fear. Fourth mile, demon of unworthiness, all of them the underlying source of the ultimate fire-breathing dragon known as anxiety. Day after day, rain or shine, shin splints and sore muscles, running had carried her through to graduation.

That early evening, as Lillian drove through Coral Gables towards her hotel, she reflected on her journey to outrun anxiety and recalled sessions with her fifteen-year-old male client named Corey. His anxiety had begun in utero. He experienced trauma when he was growing in his mother's womb and then witnessed his mother beaten by his father, in vicious cycles, from birth until he was five years old. There were some good days, but when things got bad, they went from bad to worse quickly. He lived among cockroaches, cigarette butts, beer bottles, and hypodermic needles.

By the time he was seven, his mother was dead, his father incarcerated, and with no willing or able relatives to take him in, he was in his second foster home. Foster care was no walk in the park for him either. As Lillian saw much too often, there were sometimes chaotic conditions, bullying among foster siblings, and authoritarian foster parents, causing trauma on top of trauma within the system. He had to process many memories with

Lillian to be able to identify the beginning source of his anxiety and then learn how to manage it, not just let it manage him.

Corey was being fostered by a loving family with three other siblings, when at the age of nine, he saw Lillian for the first time. His foster parents had fallen in love with him and wanted to adopt him, but they were worried about behavioral issues that were surfacing. His pediatrician was too quick to label him Attention Deficit Hyperactivity Disorder (ADHD), Combined Type, challenged with both hyperactivity and inattention, and he started psychostimulants. Like so many dysregulated children that came through Lillian's office, it was when the psychostimulants didn't work that Lillian uncovered past trauma with her clients. Then she was able to provide them with psychoeducation that helped them understand that ADHD symptoms often mimic trauma symptoms, and trauma must be ruled out first. Medication was not needed in this case; trauma-focused therapy was the remedy. Corey also had to replace the "bad cycle" stuck in his head with the "good cycle." The bad cycle told him that something bad had happened to him, which meant that he was bad, which caused him to act bad, and so he deserved to be treated bad. The good cycle reminded him that something bad happened to him, but he was good, could make good decisions, and deserved to be treated good.

Lillian fell in love with Corey too. If there was ever a client to get her to quit her job so she could adopt him herself, it was Corey. Play therapy techniques, used to build rapport early in sessions, revealed evidence of physical abuse by one of his previous foster parents. Lillian's heart sank as she called the abuse hotline after his session one late afternoon. She was supposed to meet Joshua for dinner at the Casa Monica restaurant. She looked forward to walking through their lobby that always smelled of chlorine from the wishing well fountain. The bathroom was the cleanest in town. It housed a gold-framed, full-length mirror to double-check your outfit on the way out. After dinner, they had planned to eat ice cream on the bayfront wall and watch the sun set. It was the time of day you could always spot a pod of dolphins moving through the bay. It was nature's gift of decompression for worn-out humans. She sent a text that she would be a little late, *client emergency, I'm okay, be there asap.* Corey's abuse call was just one of dozens of abuse calls throughout her career so far. She loathed the dark world.

Chapter 55

L illian had brought out the big guns for Corey—Trauma-Focused
Cognitive Behavioral Therapy (TF-CBT), which included creation of
a mental safe place through guided imagery. A safe place was a protected
place in his mind that he could temporarily escape to when trauma reminders got too intense. He already had been actively participating in play and
art therapy techniques, including sand tray play. She offered a strengths-
based focus and at the end he completed a trauma narrative using her finger puppets. Conjoint parent and child sessions allowed his pre-adoptive
parents to learn about trauma, their role in his healing process, and to
solidify their family bond. Corey eventually came back to see Lillian at age
fifteen, brought by his adoptive mother.

"For the most part, he has been doing so well! He just seems to need
some refreshers and reminders. He seems more anxious and restless than
ever, like he was when he first came to live with us. He has his driving per-
mit now but has such bad driving anxiety, we can't get him to leave the
driveway." She explained. "I remember you saying that when he reaches
milestones, like puberty, adulthood, marriage, parenthood, he may require
therapy to process memories in a new light. And that, sometimes, things
may come up that his brain had not been ready to process yet as a child,
but would be, as he grew older and could handle it. I think we're at that first
milestone."

Corey greeted Lillian with a bear hug. She never initiated hugs with
clients. But when a client reached out to her, especially a child, she recipro-
cated if they had already built rapport. A child who had experienced abuse
especially needed that validation. It served as another reminder that said,

I am a safe person in your life. This is what healthy love feels like. Lillian looked up at Corey as she stepped back from him.

"Corey! Look at you! So tall and grown," she proclaimed. Corey, who used to trip on his shoelaces, would come to sessions drinking juice boxes, and had temper tantrum meltdowns often in the beginning or at the end of sessions. But there he stood, towering over Lillian, almost six feet tall with a smile that was larger than life.

"Hi, Ms. Lillian. I'm fifteen now," Corey offered.

It took ten weeks of sessions for Corey to process new abuse flashbacks that were causing anxiety and anger outbursts. Corey's symptoms manifested as an inability to focus and complete tasks, some academic slips, decreased self-esteem, issues on the football field with fellow players, impatience with his siblings, and an avoidance of responsibilities. He would rather stay lost in video games and binge-watch television shows. His driving anxiety was an underlying issue of lack of control; he was an overly defensive driver and thinker. He would foresee accidents at every turn and anticipated cars ramming him or braking too soon. Lillian walked him back through the steps of TF-CBT, revisiting his mental safe place that he then added to with his fifteen-year-old brain. She also had reviewed his faith beliefs, which were one of his identified strengths. She was able to reframe his defensive-driving brain as a good thing and showed him how it could be a strength instead of a weakness.

Corey, who created a sweet, sad, and honest trauma narrative when he was nine years old, with finger puppets, now chose to create a rap song that exemplified his adolescent journey. The rap featured new insights that he had gained his second time through the therapy process, six years later.

Chapter 56

Lillian smiled when she thought back to that therapy graduation session. She had brought out her giant bubble-blowing set and bracelet kit. His favorite colors chosen for his bracelet were green and black. She engaged all her child abuse survivor clients in this graduation ritual of blowing the bubbles up into the sky with deep, controlled breaths to represent letting go. They would sit in the grass and watch the bubbles float up and away as she reminded them of their strengths and all they had overcome. Then they created a bracelet together, using the child's two favorite colors and the color yellow, always added by Lillian. Yellow represented the hope that their abuse did not define them, and that they would be a light in the world because they overcame the darkness thrust upon them.

"Okay, Ms. Lillian. I've been practicing. I'm so ready. Are you ready?" he asked as he stood up in her office and rocked back and forth to a beat in his head.

"I'm so ready, Corey!" she emphasized as she mimicked his motion and gave him center stage. His adoptive parents sat side by side, prepared for their son's creative expression of his pain. His mother already had tears welling in her eyes. Her heart overflowed with a love that could not have been more if she had birthed him herself.

"I didn't ask to be born into the dark,
I didn't deserve to watch my momma get marked.
All I wanted was a daddy that could keep me safe,
But he let the demons in, and they overtake our place.
Now my momma in Heaven and my daddy in jail,

I was an orphan, with a heavy dark tale.
The pain that was put on me, was from the enemy,
He tried to steal my life; that devil lied to me.
Ms. Lillian taught me how to say how I feel,
The system brought me a family to help me heal.
No matter where I been or what happened to me,
I'm anointed and adopted in God's family.
I'm anointed and adopted in God's family.
I'm not done, I'm not done, I'm just getting started and I'm ready to run.
I'm not done, I'm not done, I'm just getting started and I'm ready for fun."

Lillian's heart had been full. The trauma Corey had endured, and his endless positive character traits, made him resilient and wise beyond his years. Despite all his suffering, he was open to God working on his behalf. Corey went on, explaining the lyrics of his rap and what they meant to him.

"How do you feel, Corey?" Lillian inquired.

"Free. Like I'm unstoppable. Like God has a great plan for my life," he replied.

Chapter 51

Once inside her hotel room in Coral Gables, Lillian turned the news on to replace the quiet in the room and distract from her inner-most thoughts. The news stations all offered updates of the storm, still not arrived, but moving slowly and strengthening. It was expected to come to shore early Saturday. The different models gave several different scenarios, but the European model showed it skirting the coast and moving away. Surely it was the one everyone was hoping for. The influx of weather information was a reminder of the love of storms that she and Joshua shared.

Throughout college, they walked to classes endless times in the warm rain. When others were secure under umbrellas or in their dorm rooms and apartments during downpours, they took front-row seats under patio umbrellas and open breezeways all over campus. Joshua added to his patio furniture to create a cozy and welcoming backyard sanctuary overlooking multiple palm trees and a man-made lake with an ever-flowing fountain in the middle.

It had been a gesture of love for Lillian so they could sit together in nature. Joshua read a devotional with her that emphasized that God reveals Himself to His people through scripture and nature. He made a conscious effort to bring Lillian glimpses of a loving, tangible God in their time together outdoors. Joshua shared with her that he believed God was every-where, though he acknowledged that some people disagreed. Others chose to reject the idea of a God, making themselves and one another gods, and still others tried to discredit Christians. Then, there was the category he suspected Lillian fit into—acknowledging and embracing that there was a God but running and attempting to hide from Him. He was convinced that she felt unworthy, forgetting her worthiness was not about what she had or hadn't done, but that it was about the Father's Son and what He already did for her. Joshua's leading was never forceful, always gentle and cautious.

So, they planted flowers together. He took her on outings to Jungle Island and borrowed a professor's boat once a month so they could float among the sea life. Sometimes they boated close to the shore or the intracoastal, other times, venturing out until the shore was barely in sight. Seeing the multi-colored parrots or spotting dolphins and shark fins were always reminders of the creative mind of God for Joshua, and his delight in sharing those encounters was never oppressive for Lillian.

"I pray that by immersing you in His beauty, Lil, that you rediscover the wonderment of God," Joshua whispered one evening while they watched the sun set on the boat stern before heading back to shore. Lillian laid between his legs. She fit perfectly. Their bodies were sun kissed and sweaty, causing chills and a dive under a blanket. They were intertwined, touching affectionately all day, but never crossing the boundary of what Joshua considered sacred. He gently kissed the scars on her foot and thumb. She didn't reply with words, only a squeeze of his hand. She took a deep breath and sat in awe that he had used that phrase—about God. She never told him she had lost the wonderment of God. The fact that he was so tuned in to her, that he could see her struggle and put the exact words to it, made her realize how much she had grown to love him.

Chapter 58

Their love of storms had one exception. They had a mutual respect for lightning and swiftly returned indoors whenever it turned up to play. Joshua had a childhood trauma memory of a teammate who had been struck by lightning and killed during a Little League baseball practice one summer when he was nine. His parents had thought bringing him back to the States for an American experience like baseball would be beneficial for him. Ultimately, he had longed to get back to the adventures of other countries. He wanted to kick the *futebol* in São Paulo, Brazil, one of his favorite places in the world, during his parents' overseas adventures. He had returned there when he was seventeen and soaked in the culture. Then he went back one more time after his parents died, as part of his healing expedition.

Joshua recalled São Paulo as an urban labyrinth, huge and colorful. The streets and metro station were crowded, making it easy to get smashed between people, but it was cleaner than any other metro he had ever seen. Joshua had always been ready to offer his seat to someone older, more vulnerable. The underground held the sounds of musicians hoping for coins to be dropped in their hats or jars and when you reentered the streets; there always seemed to be a lady dressed in fancy clothes trying to read your hand.

Joshua recollected a beautiful, petite, pale-skinned girl he met there, named Laura, but known as *"La-La"* to her friends. She had large, beautiful brown eyes, the obvious windows to her soul. She liked to color her long, naturally dark hair for fun—sometimes red, sometimes pink, or blue.

She had shown all the beauty and different features of her country to him, beyond what any tourist guide could offer.

There was a church or bar on every corner. Large, mirrored buildings filled the financial district. Restaurants and hot dog stands, offering mashed potatoes with corn and bacon inside, were packed at lunchtime. Hard workers enjoying their mid-day breaks had many food options. You could enjoy falafel in Arab restaurants owned by families from Cear`a. Thousands of self-serve restaurants provided a huge variety of rice, beans, feijoada, salads, and every possible dish to be made with mandioca. Joshua had loved to wash his meals down with acerola juice or a cold beer.

Back then, walking within neighborhoods meant uneven sidewalks and many colorful iron gates that held back dogs who barked to protect their territory when you walked by. Unfortunately, you had to be diligent, with keys close, especially at night, because criminals lurked in the shadows awaiting their moment of opportunity. Joshua had enjoyed many novellas with La-La as he visited her home. He did not understand Portuguese, only a few words, but it made a beautiful sound when it fell off their tongues. La-La revealed that she had been born on the day of the dead, November 2. She was proud to have been born on "all souls day." It was her pleasure to celebrate her birth on the day they celebrated the memory of the dead. She had many painted skulls in her room to remind her to live life to the fullest, that death was around the corner and, although it was nothing to fear, you did not want to fall short of your purpose on earth while alive.

La-La's family had welcomed him the entire time he was there. He shared in their tradition to jump seven waves and make seven wishes in Rio de Janeiro one New Year, a tradition with deep roots brought from the continent of Africa. Brazil was a country where a high percentage of people embraced Catholicism, but 100% embraced spiritualism.

There were no boundaries for the Brazilians in their family gatherings and parties. Everyone kissed, danced, and enjoyed every moment because "you did not know what tomorrow would bring." They did not have time or worry for modesty, Joshua learned. Different shades of skin were illuminated by the moon, sweating, shown through low-cut dresses and short shorts. *They had a right to be vain,* Joshua thought. They were beautiful people with beautiful traditions. Brazil was where Joshua had learned how to chill, love, and live.

Chapter 59

W hile Joshua's memories of lightning ranged from American baseball to Brazilian beauty, Lillian's turned to the north and a vivid storm memory that had resulted in another moment in time with Jeremiah. The experience of racing to her grandparents' garage on her four-wheeler during a lightning storm was another wild adventure notch she had scratched into her bedpost. It was the same summer she ran into the badminton net and bloodied her face. She was too deep in the woods when the storm rolled in and she had sped to get home. While trying to beat it back, a weak tree nearby was struck by lightning, causing it to fall right in front of her path. She veered quickly to the left, hitting a pothole, overturning the vehicle, and sending pain shooting through her left wrist. It also left a burn mark down her left inner calf muscle. With a lot of determination and adrenaline spiked by trauma, she was able to turn the four-wheeler upright and get it home to the detached garage. She laid on the cot near her grandfather's workbench, waiting out the fury of the storm before sheepishly walking into the main house. She had to find dry clothes and two ice packs, one for her wrist and one for her leg. She remembered feeling thankful her throwing arm was intact, anticipating the upcoming softball season.

As she turned from the freezer with the ice, she jumped just a little at the sight of her grandfather sitting at the kitchen table in the dark. The only glow in the room was provided by the dim light above the stove and occasional lightning flashes. She shouldn't have been so surprised. It was his late-evening tradition. He would sit with a piece of fruit, usually an apple or a peach. The apples were from their very own apple orchard a few miles down a long, winding country road. That was where Lillian practiced driving her grandfather's truck, in between the rows, unbeknownst to her parents. Their delicious little secret. He would smile with pride.

"You are full of Sisu, Lillian," he would declare. It was a Finnish word used to describe a strong character of bravery and determination. She would climb to the highest part of the trees and, remarkably, never seemed to injure herself there. There was never a need for dinner after apple-picking days, her stomach full of all her samplings.

He would always carve thin pieces with a sharp knife and enjoy the healthy snack while going over his chores for the following day. Slicing, eating, slicing, eating. Always being mindful to not allow the sharp blade to touch his lips.

"Want a piece?" he asked. She sat down, nodding, and received the next slice. Her hair was soaked and stringy, covering her face. She pushed back just enough to get the fruit in her mouth. Grandfather must have been extra hungry that night. He had an apple and a peach. The sweet juice provided by the peach was welcomed. She closed her eyes and sucked on it before chewing.

"Want to talk about it?" he inquired as he examined her from head to toe. She shook her head and they sat in silence. He leaned over, gave her shoulder a tender squeeze, smiled gently, and cut another slice. It was as if he relentlessly believed in her, no matter what she did, no matter what happened. No discussion would be forced; he just sat non-judgmental, quietly loving her. They watched the storm and finished the peach together; she would always drop her hand and offer Benji a piece under the table.

Chapter 60

The next day, the storm a distant memory, she asked Jeremiah to play catch with her, as they had done numerous times. Her injured wrist was her catching hand. She had wrapped it snuggly with a bandage and felt she could manage through the pain. She was working on her throw to second base as a catcher, knowing high school softball team tryouts her upcoming freshman year would be more competitive than anything she had experienced yet. Her quick setup and arm strength to second base were good, but she had to throw sidearm to achieve accuracy. Her grandfather was worried what four years of sidearm might do and suggested she work on accuracy with an overhead motion. Jeremiah played baseball in high school and was the perfect partner to get Lillian ready.

Jeremiah noticed the wrap on her wrist and the gauze on her leg that appeared to have blood seeping through it.

"What did you do this time, girl?" he had asked as he dropped his baseball glove and walked over to her.

"I flipped the four-wheeler yesterday during the storm," she replied with a grin. He stared at her; his eyes said a thousand things, but he only asked four questions and made one command.

"Did you tell anyone? Did you hit your head? Lose consciousness? Did you wash the wound? You know what, never mind, come on," he had insisted. Jeremiah grabbed her by her right hand, scooped up his baseball glove, and led her to his grandfather's house. He motioned for her to sit down at the kitchen table, took the bandage off her leg, and cleaned the wound thoroughly. He unwrapped her wrist, checked it over, and rewrapped it better than she had done by herself. He applied new gauze to her leg and placed another wrap over it to secure it. The whole time he just smiled a calm, unsurprised smile.

She studied his fingers and strong hands as he easily seemed to find the perfect balance between fixing her up securely and being delicate with the injuries. She imagined what it would feel like to be touched by him in other places. They were good butterflies, not anxious ones, that began fluttering in her stomach. She watched some beads of sweat on his forehead and above his upper lip, imagining the sweet and salty taste she'd find there. She closed her eyes and leaned in slightly. Jeremiah was concentrating, so he was unaware of her fantasies going on literally right in front of his face.

"You need to be more careful. I'm going to be worried about you starting high school. It's a jungle out there, Lil. If you can't stay injury-free on a quiet northern property in the woods, how are you going to manage high school downstate in a big city?" he asked urgently, with genuine concern in his voice. There was no response, so Jeremiah looked up to find a dazed, fantasizing Lillian who immediately snapped out of it, opening her eyes and leaning back.

"I guess you'll just have to move down and keep an eye on me," she replied.

"Ha, that would surely be a full-time job," he replied with laughter. They ate ice cream together that day, sharing the same favorite coffee flavor, and then went back to playing catch. Lillian had been able to perfect her forward motion accuracy before she left that summer. As a freshman that fall, in a new city, surrounded by new people, where she had to prove herself, she had been promoted to varsity before the end of the first season. She also became the first-string catcher the following year, thanks to the patience and attention of Jeremiah the summer before. Amazingly, she threw out 100% of runners that had attempted to steal second base.

Chapter 61

In the hotel in Coral Gables, Lillian stretched out on the bed, kicked off her shoes, and closed her eyes. She still had not told Joshua about Jeremiah, fifteen years later, since their first date. She realized now with alarming clarity, in the quiet of the hotel room, that she had yet to fully open her heart to her husband. Jeremiah was one of the few men who had loved her right. She had been clinging to that image, setting a high standard for all of the men who followed him. But maybe now it was time to let him go. Perhaps he was the man who had paved the way for Lillian to allow the good and right love of Joshua to enter her heart, and she owed it to Joshua to let him be the one man who had her heart, alone. Guilt and shame surfaced. Those feelings, combined with the brewing storm off the coast, brought flooding memories of her client, Amabelle, a sweet, God-loving teenager who had recounted in their sessions her own details of a stormy night.

The referral had arrived in an encrypted email from a colleague who was a counselor at the local high school. She had thought Amabelle could use an off-campus therapist who specialized in trauma to process her story. The reason for referral read: Sexual assault, Depression, Rule out PTSD. Lillian's heart sunk when her colleague had called to give her a heads-up last spring.

"This girl had the whole world ahead of her, Lil. Top of her class, basketball team captain, well-liked, straight As, then a sexual assault by someone who walked right in her sliding back door, when she was home alone sleeping on the couch, shattered her world. Her parents are really worried about her. I planned with her teachers to have her finish the semester at home. She needs your trauma lens, Lil. You've got to bring her back," she explained.

Lillian remembered calling Amabelle's parents immediately and clearing a block of time to get her in for intake that same week. She blocked two hours so she could have her parents sign consents, gain the background information from their perspective, and begin to build rapport with Amabelle in the most gentle and delicate way. She brought out the big guns for Corey, but for Amabelle, she brought out the missiles. She knew her first task was to assess safety. She would administer a depression scale and trauma symptom checklist to get a baseline. *Was she suicidal; was she safe?*

Chapter 62

"I love God, but I don't understand why He allowed this to happen to me. I mean, I don't mean to sound like I'm above hardship, but I also don't feel like I needed some kind of a wake-up call," were the first words out of Amabelle's mouth during her intake session with Lillian. She presented with flat affect and congruent mood. She had known God in her heart since she could remember, she explained. She kept a piece of the Noah's Ark border in her scrapbook that once lined her nursery as an infant. Colorful rainbows surrounded her infancy and toddler years, reminding her of God's promise to never flood the earth again. She had made a conscious decision to tell herself out loud every time she saw a rainbow, *God always keeps His promises.*

Then, coming to Lillian at the age of seventeen, she appeared strong in her faith. A leader among her friends, captain and point guard of her basketball team, ministry bound, she proclaimed to be God's hands and feet, eager to live her life for Him. Choosing to save her virginity for her wedding night, protecting and respecting her treasure and living each day with integrity, was her choice to be true to who she was. Lillian recognized Amabelle felt confident that the duplicity that suffocated the secular world had no chance to penetrate through her solid foundation.

She expressed that she looked forward to marrying a man who put Christ first, one who would be the spiritual leader of her home, protecting her—a godly man like Boaz from the Bible. Boaz was a compassionate, observant protector and provider, a man of integrity who believed in the Lord; he was on fire for God. For Amabelle, nothing could be more attractive than that. They would have two boys and two girls, and they would pick biblical names, of course. She could just imagine them, embracing for hours on the couch, investigating God's word for just the right namesake. This would be after serving the Lord together for five years, traveling, and building orphanages and schools for Third World countries. Yes, she had it all figured out. She said she felt it in her heart that it was all God's will.

It had been an unusually warm March, the spring of Amabelle's junior year of high school. Even though it was North Florida, and being warm was the norm, the radiating heat had given spring fever to everybody way too soon. She and her classmates struggled to finish assignments and stay awake in afternoon classes, and they found themselves daydreaming about summer romance, vacations, and ruling the school as seniors next year. Her basketball team, with her leadership, was sure to use all their talent to take their team to state.

Chapter 63

Despite the tempting taste of what was to come, Amabelle did her best to stay on task. She did what she always did on Fridays, heading west after school to visit her grandfather at the nursing home, twenty minutes outside of town. She took it upon herself to visit him once a week, on her own, after she got her driver's license. It meant a lot to her father. It was difficult for him to see his father in such an incoherent state of mind. The Alzheimer's had robbed him of any trace of a prior life and the memories that came with it. Amabelle did not visit him just to lighten the load for her dad though; she really loved seeing her *papa*, as she called him. It was her pleasure, she always reassured him.

She cherished the papa she once knew, the one to whom she owed her deep faith and relationship with Jesus Christ. She would sit and read to him, review the names of the people in the pictures surrounding his bed, and pretend they were having lucid two-way conversations. Sometimes they did. He still had some moments of recognition that Amabelle, her brother, and parents would hold onto when they could get them. She told him all about school, the desire to go to state playoffs with her team in the winter, and her hopes and plans for the summer.

"Can you believe I'm going to be a senior, Papa?" Then she'd answered for him, "Wow, Ama, I'm so proud of you. I told you that you can do anything through Jesus." That is what papa had taught her; he also emphasized that her faith was about a relationship with Jesus, not religious rituals, laws, or rules. Too many churches got it wrong too often. At the time, she had not known just how much that concept would mean to her healing process post-trauma, until she wrote a trauma narrative with Lillian during her last month of therapy.

One of twelve children, papa had found God as a young boy and held on to his convictions despite the fact that his siblings denounced all things religious. To that day, of the remaining seven brothers and sisters still living, her papa and the generations connected to him were the only ones claiming and declaring the message of salvation. Amabelle prayed for her distant relatives, imagining them in a miserable afterlife, separated from God forever. Oh, how she prayed for them. She pondered why her papa, the one who accepted Christ, was the one who lost his mind. He could be out there doing more for the unsaved. Didn't he deserve more? His body was still healthy, yet he was wasting away in a nursing home, unaware of anything going on around him. It did not make sense to her, but she trusted God had a plan.

Or was this a blessing? she had contemplated. How did they know what was going on inside of his mind and dreams? Was he communicating with Jesus while receiving physical rest? Maybe sorting things out as he was preparing to go live with God? Are the ones who lose their minds set aside? Are they in a deeper spiritual realm than we can imagine? She often stared into his eyes for several minutes at a time, looking for a glimpse of paradise in there.

"Papa, do you hear Jesus? Is He in there with you?" she urged. Papa had flat affect but sometimes he smiled or, at least, she wanted him to, so she maintained that he did. The doctors tended to give scientific explanations to possible smiles, but Amabelle believed deeper than that. People are always so quick to shrug off the spiritual. We are spiritual beings, just as we are biological, psychological, and social, after all.

Chapter 64

L illian continued to listen, session after session, as Amabelle shared pieces of her life leading up to her great trauma. Amabelle had gotten all her homework done in study hall that average, muggy Friday. She had anticipated a weekend of watching her favorite movies and updating her journal entries for the week. She journaled to move her feelings out of her soul and give them a voice, to express her inner thoughts. She also kept a husband journal. She wrote down her thoughts and feelings to her future husband and planned to give it to him after he had proposed. She took some heat for her spirituality at the public school she attended, but she didn't care. She lived to please God, not man.

She was the first student at the weekly Fellowship of Christian Athletes meetings held before school. Her parents had always felt bad that they couldn't afford a private Christian school for Amabelle. She reassured them that God had her right where He wanted her. She was the salt and light in a non-Christian environment, where she could serve God even more. Her parents openly expressed how grateful they were for the unselfish and mature daughter that God had given them.

That particular weekend had been especially exciting for Amabelle because her parents were going away to a couples' retreat with friends from church. Her big brother had an out-of-town college baseball game. Although she hated missing his games, and he hated missing hers, they had a pact to do everything possible to be at every home game for each other, she relished the infrequent weekends of total solitude.

She remembered thinking how she would have the house to herself. She would take such pleasure in playing house. She'd cook herself dinner, dance across the hardwood floors, pretend she was the homeowner falling asleep on the couch. Oh, how she loved that couch! She still laughed out loud recollecting the day she and her mom found the "deal of the century." The beautiful microfiber, crimson, L- shaped sectional had sat mispriced in the middle of the furniture store showroom. Unnoticed and ignored by hurried shoppers but standing out like a neon sign to Amabelle and her mom was the red extravagance. The price tag accidently had been swapped with a clearance chair. Per their own policy, the store had to give the eight-person, oversized divan away for less than half of what it was worth. They almost felt guilty taking such a steal, until it was delivered and fit perfectly in their inviting family room. Even Amabelle's dad, who was basically colorblind and uninterested in the complications of decorating and room coordination, was more than pleased with the money his wife had saved them.

Chapter 65

Nothing had been different about the day tragedy had crept nefariously into Amabelle's prearranged life. It stole in through the sliding glass door shortly after 1 a.m., uninvited, a sinister manifestation preying on the vulnerable and innocent. She forgot to lock the door after letting her English bulldog, Bert, out for his bedtime bathroom break. He was named from her favorite British chimney sweep, in her favorite childhood movie, *Mary Poppins*.

Amabelle and Bert had been nestled tightly together in the fleece blanket in the family room, unaware of the plotting eyes that had been watching them since sundown, from the darkest corner of the backyard. Bert, just a puppy, was a round white and brown surprise Christmas gift from Amabelle's parents. He was still growing and finding his way in the family. He enjoyed eating, snuggling, and sleeping more than playing watchdog but clearly identified Amabelle as his person. He followed her around throughout the house and waited for her return when she left the premises.

It had begun raining around 8 p.m. and continued throughout the late-night hours and into early morning. The rainfall and occasional thunder clang created a rhythmic symphony that aided in her relaxation and sleepiness.

She had been in a deep dream where she'd been sitting on a dock at the athletic summer youth camp she went to every year. The experience of connection with a group of like-minded, soul-linked people brought her to tears every summer. The sun was warm, shining down on her, bringing a deepened color to her already dark-tanned, strong, lean legs. The lake water that barely touched her toes was warm and murky. She stretched to allow her feet to submerge like she had done a hundred times at camp before. If she had been awake instead of dreaming, she probably would have pulled back quickly, her imagination getting the best of her, sure a fish might take a nibble at her toes. But in the dream, which was so vivid, she had no fear, she lowered herself into the water and swam freely, smiling, allowing the bright sun to kiss her face.

After a few moments, she noticed a figure on the opposite shore watching her. She was curious, but still fearless. At the same time, she heard howling from the woods. Still not realizing she was in a dream and anything could happen, she didn't feel uneasy about the wolves. If she had been awake, she would have thought it was odd to hear wolves during the day. In every storybook she had ever read or movie she had watched, wolves howled at night, especially in the presence of a full moon. Amabelle was gently treading water and enjoying the sunshine. Then, slowly, the light evolved into a creeping darkness that brought the movement of clouds over the sun. She felt trapped and began to panic and swam in fear.

Quickly, wolves surrounded the shore and dock. She couldn't see a way to safety and her arms were getting tired. The figure across the lake, who appeared male, stood there with arms stretched out. There were no wolves near him, as if he had an invisible force field; they did not come within several feet on all sides. She started to swim towards him, but as she swam, more heavy fear engulfed her. She felt herself sinking and with a final thought, *this is it, I'm going to die*, she surrendered, exhausted, to the lake's pull.

Amabelle woke up from the drowning dream with a jolt, gasping for air, as a dark figure was standing over her. She screamed. A tall, broad-chested male wearing dark clothes and a ski mask was quickly on top of her. He placed his hand over her mouth.

"*Shut up!*" he demanded. Amabelle, a strong athlete, fought. She bit into two of his fingers and he punched her hard across her left cheek, causing a sting and then ringing in her head, unlike any sports injury she had ever experienced. Bert yelped as the man tossed him across the room with his other hand. Despite the pain in her head, she swung her fists then thrust her pelvis up to try to shake him off her.

Her fight only seemed to excite him, as he laughed, moaned, and over-powered her. Just as soon as it began, it seemed, it was over. It could have been minutes or hours though. Amabelle disassociated. What began as *fight* in this fight-flight-or-freeze human predicament, ended in *freeze*. As he had worked his pants down and pushed inside of her, the initial pain of penetration and thrusting turned into numbness. In swift minutes, he stole what was most precious to her, her virginity, the gift she was treasuring for her future husband.

He exited out the sliding door just as stealthily as he had entered. Amabelle rolled over onto the floor, off the couch, and crawled to the door, sliding it fully closed and locking it. Bert, with a gentle cry, hiding under her father's favorite reading chair, made his way to her face and offered puppy kisses. She pulled him into her while laying on her side in the fetal position on the floor. She squinted her eyes and zeroed in on the flash of red basketball shoes walking away.

Chapter 66

Reaching for science, like a comfortable blanket, using TF-CBT techniques once again, step-by-step with fidelity, Lillian was able to move Amabelle from a state of textbook post-traumatic stress disorder to a place of healing in four months. The sessions started first with two times per week, then stepped down to once per week. The fact that her parents had believed her and supported her helped her in leaps and bounds. Lillian thought first of Sadie and then other clients whose sufferings were heaped on top of trauma when their "safe people" did not believe their revealed experience.

Here she was again, assisting a client in creating a mental safe place using all five of their senses. This was one of her favorite therapy techniques. It was most important to provide a client with the method prior to processing past hurt. It was a tool they could take with them and use anytime at home, school, or work. If emotions or memories became too intense, a visit to their created safe world, in their mind, would offer relief and comfort. Something that was so easy with Corey proved to be more challenging with Amabelle.

There were two rules. First, you could not mentally place any other human being there with you because humans are not always safe. Second, you had to agree to always return from your mental safe place back to reality. You could not stay there indefinitely. Lillian remembered how she gently prompted during her second session with Amabelle.

"Close your eyes and slowly breathe through your nose, four-second count in, hold for four, four-second count out through your nose, relax for four. Move your breath into your extremities. Feel your right arm relaxing heavily into the couch, now your left. Feel your right leg relaxing heavily into the couch, now your left. Gently and kindly place your thoughts into an imaginary jar for later and clear your brain like you are erasing a dry-erase board. Breathe in positivity, breathe out negativity. Now I want you to imagine the safest, most beautiful place you can think of and put yourself there alone. Maybe you are on a mountain, on the beach, near a river, at a park, or in a meadow. Breathe in, breathe out. Take your time. Tell me where you are." Lillian paused and patiently waited Amabelle's response.

"I'm near a lake," Amabelle shared.

"Describe what you see," Lillian encouraged. Amabelle stopped and opened her eyes.

"I can't. I keep having images of the same nightmare, and all I see are the wolves," she asserted.

Recognizing that Amabelle was not ready to create a mental safe place, Lillian had paused. She encouraged her to open her eyes and focus on breathing in and out slowly and deeply through her nose to calm her central nervous system. She prompted her to identify and name objects in the room to help her stay grounded.

"The interpretation of the dream is up to the dreamer, Amabelle. Continue to write down what you remember as soon as you wake up and bring your dream journal to sessions. We will process them and look for patterns or themes, but it is up to you to determine what your mind or your God is trying to tell you while you sleep," Lillian explained. It had required Amabelle keeping a dream journal by her bed and three more weeks of sessions to finally process her dream. It had continued to evolve. Then they had to find a message in it and prepare her to move forward with her trauma work.

It was a cloudy afternoon with off-and-on rain showers when Amabelle had shared her revelation. Lillian lit a candle and turned on several lamps to restore the energy in the room from a lack of sunlight. Amabelle pulled the blanket provided on the back of the couch over her lap and nestled into it.

"I think I understand my dream now. God was letting me know that something bad was coming but I am not alone. One of the wolves represents my rapist. But there are many wolves; the rest represent the darkness in the world that will always be around, preying, lurking. By keeping my eyes on Jesus, I don't drown—I swim and make it over to Him. He's waiting on the shore. I find comfort and rest there. The wolves watch, but they can't get close to Him, so I'm safe," she affirmed.

Amabelle said she realized that living for God did not set her apart from tragedy. In fact, her devotion to Him would open her up to more persecution; it was promised. She did not do anything to deserve to be raped and by God allowing it, it did not mean she was loved less or abandoned by Him. There was evil in the world, and time on earth was just a vapor. Her identification of the red basketball shoes, and the rain and mud, helped the police find a perfect shoe imprint of her assailant. He had been stalking her from the corner of the backyard, and the print led the detectives to question and receive a confession from a boys' varsity basketball player. Sadly, Amabelle learned he'd been addicted to pornography and had become obsessed with her Christian, moral standards.

Thankfully, Amabelle came to realize, there would be no negative memories or trauma triggers in Heaven. Looking at her experience through eternal eyes, instead of temporal eyes, allowed her to see that with her faith and God-given strengths, she could endure the rape and watch good unfold from it. She could use her testimony to help others, but the journey to get there had been dark and painful. It required her parents throwing away the favored couch where the assault took place. They all repainted and redecorated the room together. But before all the healing, there were some dark and difficult days when she had contemplated suicide and needed to be Baker Acted, Florida's involuntary admittance at the local psychiatric hospital for assessment and observation.

Chapter 67

Lillian saw Amabelle within twenty-four hours of her Baker Act release. She looked a little paler and thinner.

"Hey, girl," Lillian said with a soft and supportive tone, as she invited Amabelle into the stillness of her office. A nod and smile to her mother had said, *I got her; she will be okay.*

"I wasn't going to kill myself, I just really wanted to be with Jesus," Amabelle had replied.

"Tell me more about that." Lillian nodded. Amabelle continued.

"I feel like I understand the mind of someone who ends their life, especially a Christian. I know that doesn't make sense. Life is a precious gift from God, and our bodies are temples. But you slip into a mindset that you don't want the pain of the evil world anymore; you just want to go home." Lillian processed this concept with Amabelle and later, when alone, reflected on the pain of her own mother's suicide.

She felt a little more understanding and forgiving towards her mother's family. She reflected on how her maternal grandmother was abandoned by her mother before her when she was only six years old, through sudden illness. She had done the best she could when raising her own daughter but had fallen short. Then her father deserted her when he hung himself from the rafters in the attic. It was a tragic family legacy failing three generations. Each offspring had faced life with baggage from the past and no roadmap for the unknown future.

Amabelle completed her trauma work with reduced symptoms and was ready for her senior year of high school by early August. Lillian kept her scheduled once per week for the first few weeks of school in case anything came up for her that she needed to process. At her last appointment, her discharge session, where she would review all her progress, her strengths, and say good-bye, Amabelle had presented with a giant smile.

"Hi! Ms. Lillian, I have so much to tell you!" Amabelle reported with excitement in her voice as she aggressively drank a white and brown venti Frappuccino through a straw.

"Amabelle, you're making that frappé look real good, girl—but I'm all ears. Talk to me," Lillian replied while she cupped her ears and sat back to listen. She could smell the vanilla and caramel. She grabbed her hot, green tea and pretended it tasted how Amabelle's drink smelled. Amabelle laughed and continued.

"I was at basketball practice the other day thinking about my trauma narrative that I wrote and read out loud to you and my parents. I was thinking about how good can come out of my experience. I don't know why, but it was like I was on autopilot. I went in the locker room and got the big container of disinfectant wipes. I asked my teammates to sit down on the bench. I started at one end, and I washed their shoes with wipes …like how Jesus washed his disciples' feet.

I told them, as their captain, "I am no better than you. I wash your feet to show you that we have to serve each other. No one is greater. We are a team." Lillian stared in astonishment. Her maturity and ability to bring that lesson to her teammates in that way impressed her.

"How did that make you feel, Amabelle? How did they respond?" she asked. Amabelle continued.

"I felt wonderful. I felt like putting the focus on them healed my heart even more, in that moment. I felt like God gave me a hug. Some of my teammates didn't understand, but they were like, 'Okay, thanks for the shoe clean.' But I just wanted to plant a seed. I know you said that not everyone will be able to handle my story or need to hear my story. This was my way of sharing a piece of me without those specific details of my trauma experience." Lillian had encouraged Amabelle with a nod. She went on.

"Also, I've been writing a lot in my husband journal. I am writing to my future husband. I tell him my hopes and fears. I write about the healthy, consensual sex that I look forward to. I write about my sadness that my virginity is gone, but that I know when my husband finds me and pursues me, he will see me clean and unblemished. It gives me comfort."

Lillian never saw Amabelle again after that day. But as a therapist, she knew, no news was good news.

Sitting in the hotel room, Lillian rubbed her head and closed her eyes. How many times had she explained to clients that you cannot tell your brain to stop thinking about something? You can't just flip a switch; you have to replace the thoughts with different thoughts. She was unable to feel settled and relaxed. Her overactive brain and waves of guilt and worry, for ignoring all of Joshua's unanswered phone calls and texts, kept her awake. Now she saw several missed calls from Hailey and a few texts from Elijah too.

"Ugh, next Elijah will have the cops out checking on me," she mumbled. She could easily answer them and eliminate all their worry. They just wanted to know how her trip was and if she had arrived safely. To them, after all, she was attending a conference. She avoided answering because she didn't want to tell one more white lie, or tweak one more truth.

Chapter 68

Rising from the bed and leaving her phone in the room, Lillian took a walk out through her sliding glass door, through the wrought iron gate, to the edge of the pool. Warm, thick air drove her to sit on the side and immerse her feet and calves in the refreshing water. She pulled her hair into a high bun, noticing the strong scent of chlorine, sure to kill all the germs provided by the guests.

There was a father lying on a patio recliner, smiling as he watched a boy and girl horseplay in the pool.

"Daddy, watch!" they called out in unison.

Like all children looking to their parent for approval and validation, the siblings captured their father's attention before racing each other from one side of the pool to the other. The brother won by two strokes, celebrating as their father cheered them both on.

"Great job!" he yelled to them both.

A woman entered the pool area through the sliding door of her room and walked over to the man, offering him a blue Solo cup and a kiss, then she called to the children.

"Hey! I missed it, do it again!" She sat down between her husband's legs with her own cup and leaned back against his chest. *No doubt filled with, what had Hannah called it? A 'drink drink' or alcoholic beverage,* Lillian thought with a smile.

"Okay, Momma this one's for you!" the son called out. As they set up to race again, Lillian noticed that the brother gave his sister a head start, unbeknownst to her, giving her an advantage and the win. She smiled to herself.

She watched the son walk quickly over to his mother and plant a kiss on her cheek. *What great parents, what a sweet boy, what a special family,* she thought to herself, each member seemingly doing their part to validate the other during precious family time. Lillian felt emotional seeing the beautiful mother-son bond and healthy family dynamics. She came from a broken family and worked with so many broken families. Witnessing their love and joy was refreshing. She overheard them talking about getting back down to Key West as soon as the hurricane passes through. *They are here for refuge. I am here for deception,* she thought as she looked away to stop invading their moment like some desperate onlooker.

The siblings and the pool setting reminded Lillian of many individual and family sessions with a family of four she had had the privilege to work with on their painful path. She moved to a pool recliner, looked up at the painted sunset with no hint of a storm churning out at sea, and reflected on her sessions. The sounds of the siblings in the pool faded as Lillian allowed the client memories to flood in as she thought, *no use fighting them now.*

Chapter 69

Kol and Katalina were ten-year-old twins. They saw her for several grief sessions, after having family sessions with their mother and father, in preparation for their mother's death. Lillian had cherished her individual sessions with their mother first. She considered it an honor to essentially prepare her to pass from this life to her next, although it was tragic and sad, and did not seem fair for her to die so young. She was only forty-three.

The morning Katherine found out she had aggressive, stage four, terminal lung cancer was the day the earth no longer rotated correctly for her. Flowers carried no smell, food was tasteless and colorless, time kept by a clock did not matter anymore, yet it was all that mattered because it would not stand still. She had two beautiful children; she was a loving mother and devoted wife; tick-tock, tick-tock. Did she have weeks? Or maybe months. Death was imminent, sooner rather than later, the doctor had stated, his voice holding a hint of emotion, or did it? It was not emotional enough, she decided. Katherine wanted to hear emotion in his voice; she wanted him to cry with her, hold her, tell her he would work around the clock to find a cure for her. She wanted him to bring her a solution to this disease eating away her breathing organ and rapidly moving on to other areas of her body.

"I'm sorry. Can we call someone for you?" he asked. Then he left the room, moving on to his next patient, with only a brief grasp of her shoulder. This did not make any sense. He had to be wrong. The tests had to be incorrect, or accidently switched with a different patient. She did everything right. Katherine made all the right choices. She had too much to live for. She was short of breath lately due to this chronic cough she could not shake, and she lost her appetite, which contributed to her cough. But that was all. Her back hurt lately, but she just needed to stretch it out. She just needed to supplement apple cider vinegar and take more vitamins. Denial consumed her thought process and gave her the strength to walk out of the office.

Katherine had been on the swim team in college. She had rejected the alcohol and drugs many of her friends danced with. She never smoked, and she carefully watched her fat intake. Her lungs were a priceless commodity that she trained and made stronger—always pushing herself harder to hold her breath longer and swim faster. Her dedication provided her a free four-year college degree and a beautiful body. She exuded confidence and turned the heads of many of her college co-eds. But Ken was the only one who turned her head.

They had married the summer after college graduation. They had ten years together, traveling, building their careers, both high school teachers and coaches, before they were blessed with twins in their early thirties. Katherine was willing to give up her hard, contoured body for the precious lives that grew inside of her.

"Besides," she always reminded herself as her stomach stretched beyond recognition, "muscle has memory. I'll get mine back!" Being pregnant was the greatest experience she had ever known. Her husband was in awe of how naturally motherhood came to her. Her world showered her with goodness, and she wanted for nothing.

Rarely did she give in to her children's pleading to have fast-food grease and carbohydrates for a meal. Once in awhile, when she was premenstrual, she would take a last-minute quick turn into the fast-food drive-thru to savor some greasy french fries. Just a moment of weakness that sometimes included a soda, but then she'd get right back on track for another three weeks or so. She always justified it by saying it was for the kids. Her husband would laugh and go along with it, all the while telling her how incredibly beautiful and sexy she was. She could eat all the french fries and drink all the soda she wanted!

Chapter 70

"Oh God. This has to be a dream, a nightmare. Wake up! Wake up! God, help me, I can't breathe!" Katherine submitted to the panic as she sat in the parking ramp of the medical building, tearing apart her purse, looking for her cell phone to call Ken. She didn't even remember the walk from the doctor's office to her car. *No*, she stopped searching her purse and decided. She couldn't tell him on the phone, or by text; it had to be in person. But he was teaching class and then had football practice today. She could not barge into his classroom and upset his students. The football team was getting ready for the big homecoming game this Friday and she didn't want to upset his players. She was strong. She could wait. She would tell him after dinner, after the kids were tucked in bed. She thought, *I can be strong if I don't speak it out loud yet.* Because she was sure that once she spoke the words out loud, she would fall apart and he would need to hold her together, to prevent her from crumbling into a thousand pieces.

Lillian had listened to Katherine's love story unfold during the first few sessions. She had enjoyed her details about her motherhood experience, and then she had witnessed the acceptance of her fate. Chemo and radiation bought her several months, but then the cancer returned with a vengeance. Katherine managed to find peace preparing for physical death—even though she would not get to experience her daughter's first menstrual period or her son's deepened voice. She would miss out on first kisses, milestone birthdays, graduations, careers, and marriages.

She would not get to grow old and be a grandmother, to see the next generation of her family come forward. She would not get to watch her husband grow old, sure that he would grow old gracefully and look even more handsome with salt and pepper hair.

"I believe in a loving God, so Heaven has to be more beautiful and amazing than we could ever fathom for Him to take me away from the beautiful things I will miss in this world," Katherine had explained to Lillian.

"Tell me more about what you mean by that," Lillian encouraged Katherine as she leaned in.

"I mean, think about it. People get so angry at God when a child dies or a young mom like me gets a death sentence, but that's because they see death as a punishment or an end. As a believer, a physical death is just the step we have to take to get to our ultimate reward, our reward of eternal life in a perfect paradise with Jesus, God, an army of angels, and our fellow believers forever and ever. We miss out on things here, but when we are there, we don't have regrets. We don't feel sad. When our believing loved ones join us, we don't have a conversation about all the things we missed because we don't have any negative emotions. We are surrounded by unconditional love, peace, and joy. I mean, in my human mind and flesh, I wish we could just go together as a family. But God chose me to go first for reasons I don't understand, and I trust Him. I don't mean in a 'drink the Kool-Aid' kind of way. I had just always hoped Jesus would come back the second time in my lifetime, so Ken and I and our kids didn't have to experience the pain of losing each other," Katherine finished with slow, soft speech.

This woman is incredible, Lillian had thought to herself as she nodded and fought back emotion. She thought about her own mother again, who chose to take her life, leaving no motherly wisdom, no reassurance, no closure.

"You have a beautiful and incredible perspective, Katherine. As your therapist, how can I help?" she followed up.

"I want to make sure Ken and the kids will be okay. I want to complete some memories for them, some video recordings, journaling, artwork. However, I want them to already have a trusting and working relationship with you, so when I do go, you can walk them through their grief," Katherine declared.

"I can do that." Lillian gulped and nodded again.

"One more thing. I feel like crying, but I hold it in around the kids. I don't know what the right thing to do is. I want to be strong," Katherine shared.

"Crying in front of them is the greatest strength you can show them. It demonstrates that showing your emotions is a good thing and it will help them show theirs. Cry oceans together, Katherine," Lillian had edged closer and shared her clinical opinion.

Chapter 71

L illian stayed in her thoughts and replayed the family sessions when she showed both Katherine and Ken how to do back drawings on the twins as a bonding activity to promote safety, relaxation, and quality time. She approached Kol, who was willing to go first, to be brave for his sister.

"Do I have your permission to touch Kol's back, Mom and Dad?" Lillian asked his parents. They both gave verbal consent.

"No one should ever touch you without permission, okay? No one should ever touch you in any area where your bathing suit covers, except your medical doctor. Do I have permission to only touch your back, Kol?" Lillian explained. Kol nodded. Lillian always used this as an opportunity to teach families about safe touch and unsafe touch while promoting a non-threatening safe room for children. She always secured the parents' permission prior to the children entering. Some caregivers were not ready or willing to be a part of these sensitive discussions.

Lillian began. She sat behind Kol, "Crisscross applesauce." He sat with his back to her on a small, soft footstool. Lillian explained that this activity would be perfect at home, at bedtime, while lying in bed, spooning. She sat so the entire family could see what she was doing. Lillian rubbed his back in a back-and-forth motion, as if cleaning a chalkboard.

"Kol, if you feel comfortable, close your eyes and listen to my voice. Breathe in and out, slow, and deep. I'm clearing your back to have a clean slate for a special drawing. Tell yourself you are safe and loved, you are safe and loved. I am drawing a giant sunshine. Now I'm drawing you standing in a field, the sun is shining down on you, and you are safe and loved. Here is your giant castle; what color should it be?" She spoke in a quiet, soft voice, just above a whisper. Kol shifted gently; he appeared excited to be able to participate in the imagery.

"Green!" he enthusiastically replied.

"Your castle is green, and you are safe and loved," Lillian affirmed him.

"A storm is coming, Kol!" she continued. She began to draw big clouds on the top part of his back. Then in a pitter-patter motion, she made rainfall using her fingertips. She drew lightning bolts and stated, "You are safe and loved. Kol, let's go inside your castle, away from the storm." She did a walking motion with her fingers, crawling across his back to his castle space. She continued through the imagery, introducing many dynamics, encouraging Kol to participate by identifying thoughts and feelings. She always reminded him that he was safe and loved. Finally, with the storm subsiding, Lillian walked Kol back out of his castle into the sunshine and asked him how he felt.

"I feel safe and loved," Kol answered confidently. The activity went on for several minutes, including many details. Once completed, Katherine had tears in her eyes, and Katalina was excited for her turn. Ken sat quietly, watching and holding his wife's hand while Katalina sat in his lap, leaning back on his chest.

Later, Katherine engaged her children in this activity for as long as she could, until her strength gave way. Then, Ken took the torch to promote as much continuity for the children as possible, to help with their loss and transition.

"I lost a tooth after the twins were born," Katherine had said to Lillian one day in therapy. "Last one on the top left. It just rotted and failed. You've heard it said, you lose a tooth for every baby? I guess since I had two babies at the same time, I only lost one; I got a deal. Cavity, root canal, crown, then it needed to be pulled. Appointment after appointment, I tried so hard to hang on to it. I contemplated getting an implant. But then I realized, every time I felt that hole back there with my tongue, it reminded me that life is temporary. All I needed in a stressful situation was to move my tongue back there and I refocused. I am so glad I never got that implant. Even though my life is shorter than many, I can say I lived my life to the fullest," Katherine admitted, rolling her tongue around her mouth to locate the spot.

In the quiet of the hospice, towards the end, Ken did the drawing on Katherine's back as Lillian had coached him to, but he placed her in her mansion in heaven, instead of an earthly castle. He re-enacted the storm, but it was a storm on Earth. It was her last storm before her passing to eternity, where there would be no more storms, where she would surely be safe and loved beyond description.

Lillian remembered how he'd told her he had wept when the nurse came in at 5:00 a.m. for rounds, put the stethoscope to Katherine's chest, and said it was nearly time. He reached out and felt that his wife's arms and legs, warm just hours before, were now cold. The only warmth was pooled around her heart, which could no longer pump blood effectively. Her body was shutting down. The nurse paused, waited, then called the time of death as 5:10 a.m., according to the clock on the wall. Ken couldn't help but check his trusty, efficient watch which displayed 5:07 a.m. He would not correct her though, and just kept that to himself—their sacred moment, the "hour of the wolf," when she passed to the arms of Father God.

In the days and weeks afterwards, he would see the numbers 507 everywhere and would often awaken at 5:07 a.m. without an alarm. That moment, occurring twice per day, would be the sixty seconds dedicated to his wife's memory for him alone, no children, no friends, no one else allowed or invited in.

"Hi, baby" or "I love you" or "I need you" or "I can't do this without you!" he would whisper. He would say exactly what he wanted to say, exactly how he felt, without consideration for someone else's feelings, and without shame or guilt.

Chapter 72

L illian's sessions with Ken were vastly different. He was angry with God and overwhelmed. He wasn't ready to say good-bye to his wife and finish raising two children on his own. He didn't have the peace his wife had found, for a long time afterwards. He came to see Lillian three days after the funeral.

"I'm angry!" he stated with clenched fists.

"I hear you, Ken. How are you managing your anger today?" Lillian validated him. She noticed his disheveled hair and the dark rings under his eyes.

"Well, today, I had a battle with the outside trash can because I could not get the lid open. So I kicked it, spilled my hot coffee all over my chest, and then put a three-inch gash in my finger from the sharp ridges of the trash can lid," he explained. Lifting his left hand to show her, his left ring finger was wrapped in several multi-colored neon Band-aids. "I couldn't find the adult Band-aids, so I had to use the twins'. Ironic that the gash is in my ring finger, huh? Representative of the pain of the loss of my marriage, perhaps?" he contemplated.

Lillian had nodded slowly and sat with him. She did not need to review the stages of grief. He knew them, and they were posted on her wall. She did not need to explain the importance of him sharing his thoughts and feelings. They talked about those for weeks in family sessions and he helped his children do it with valiant outcomes. He did not need her to reframe a scenario or point him to a spiritual awakening—been there, done all that. She had just listened as Ken went on to share a haunting memory, with a safe person, in a safe room.

"I never knew what the 'old man's death rattle' meant that I had heard about in movies and had read about in books. I never expected that awful noise would ever come out of my wife one day. It haunts me. The way her breath crackled from the buildup of mucus and saliva. She was too weak to clear her throat. The nurse helped me shift her and give her some relief. She reassured me that she was not in any pain, that her body was slowing down, and she had peace," he had described as he stared off, beyond Lillian, reliving that painful moment.

Lillian facilitated a few more weeks of sessions with Ken, Kol, and Katalina. Most of the work had already been done before their mother left physically. Ken had to revisit the death rattle daily until it no longer haunted him but instead became a familiar and nonthreatening memory of the last days. He accepted that his earthly journey with his wife by his side was over, and he knew he would see her again when God called him home. He had learned the greatest of lessons for those who grieve: working through the pain, being willing to stand in it and experience it whenever it arrived, while reaching to embrace the joy of your life that is happening right in front of you. He was learning to live in both emotions simultaneously and not trying to push one or the other away.

Chapter 73

Lillian walked to her destination Friday morning, the same women's clinic she had gone to when she was eighteen. It was only two buildings down from her Coral Gables hotel. *Here I am again,* she thought to herself. *Right on time for my 8:30 a.m. appointment.* How many times had she helped clients identify destructive patterns in their own lives, and here she was living out her own? Several women were seated around the perimeter of the waiting room, quiet and reserved. The room was cold and smelled sterile, mostly of hand sanitizer. Outdated magazines were stacked in disheveled piles around the room, as if no one cared about their relevance. They were just a decoration to provide some faux comfort. No one was looking through them and no one was looking up to make eye contact either, except Lillian. Eye contact was her profession. It was how she could read people and navigate their souls. *Someone look at me. Someone say something,* she willed with her mind.

She glanced at the magazine cover sitting directly in front of her, as time slowly crept by. The handsome man on the cover of one of them reminded her of her client, Isaac, her gay client who struggled with his family's acceptance of his sexual orientation. Her mind flashed through memories of their individual and family sessions.

Isaac grew up going to church and worshiping God. He had fond memories of Bible camp, learning songs and performing skits. When he realized he was sexually attracted to men, not women, his world became complicated. So much of Lillian's work was predominantly with Isaac's parents. They were unable to accept their son's sexual orientation, holding onto hopes of watching him walk his bride down the aisle one day.

"This is not right. I don't understand!" exclaimed his mother in one session, as Lillian patiently allowed her the safety to express her pain and frustration.

Lillian had several sessions with Isaac to process his frustration, but she had to have double, if not more, sessions with his parents. She had entered Isaac's world and asked him several questions. He was forthcoming and articulate.

"Have you considered that you have accepted your sexual orientation, but you need to be a little more patient with them? They need to grieve the loss of their idea of who they think their son should be. They need to grieve the fact that they won't see you walk down the aisle with a wife. That is a lot for them, Isaac," she proposed.

"This has been a lot for me! I'm so tired of worrying about everyone else's perspective. I've hidden who I am from them long enough. I'm so tired of tiptoeing around my family and waiting for God to punish me. I refuse to believe in a punishing God." He raised his voice for the first time in session. He proclaimed his innermost feelings.

"There it is," Lillian responded.

"There's what?" he asked.

"Your voice. When do you think you'll be ready to say that to Mom and Dad?" she asked.

"I guess I'm ready now," Isaac realized with a smile and tears that represented too many years of suppression.

So many of her LGBTQ+ clients were not in need of interpersonal therapy as much as they needed help interacting with their people. They just wanted and needed to be who they felt they were, to be true to themselves. It was their loved ones who needed the most therapy. Lillian found herself repeating the same words to many family members over the years.

"Are you willing to lose a relationship with your son or daughter over an idea of who you think they should be or how you think things should be?" she would ask. Then the theology struggle would surface.

"It's against God. It's an abomination!" caregivers would proclaim. Lillian heard it from parents of faith, time and time again. They didn't realize the irony of being first willing to lose a relationship with their loved one for their faith convictions, but then also becoming the very obstacle that would turn that loved one away from God and the church.

"You cannot accept what they do or how they feel, but can you love them? Can you accept that they are a child of God and leave their choice between them and God? Can you accept that you were chosen to be your child's parent, but ultimately, they belong to God, and your role is to show them love?" she reminded them. Then to her clients, "You are more than your sexual orientation or gender identity. There are so many facets of you! You are also a son, daughter, brother, sister, friend. Don't lose sight of 'the all of you' while fighting for this significant piece of you." Lillian fought back emotion when she remembered Isaac and his parents' final family session.

"I love you and I choose to accept you, son. I will continue to embrace and practice acceptance every day of my life," his mother declared with open body language and steady eye contact. His father, less verbal, but present to symbolize solidarity, nodded in agreement. It's exactly what Isaac longed for.

Chapter 74

A young, female nurse spoke Lillian's name and gestured for her to come with her. *This is it,* Lillian thought. Joshua was not going to rescue her, not this time. She had not even given him a chance. She asked to use the bathroom on the way back and the nurse led her down a long hallway. Lillian closed the door and stared back at herself in the mirror. The thoughts of self-loathing and internal persecution that she had worked so hard on many years ago, and that Joshua had helped reduce to a background whisper, returned with a thunderous roar.

She heard commotion outside the bathroom door but found no one there to direct her when she exited the room. Unsure where to go, she tentatively began to walk down the hallway. As she peered into a room adjacent to the bathroom, she saw blood covering the floor and medical tools. There was a blood-stained sheet that had been left lying over the gynecological examination table. Lillian suddenly felt nauseous and light-headed. Her vision blurred, and her skin seemed to get clammy all of a sudden. With voices down the hall becoming muffled and then nearly inaudible, she felt disoriented. She felt she was entering a tunnel and that the world was closing in on her. *Just breathe,* she told herself. Thoughts of her own individual counseling sessions, that she'd been attending for weeks without telling anyone, began to flood her mind.

Chapter 15

Her therapy sessions were always following a morning run through downtown St. Augustine. With her hair pulled back in a ponytail or tucked through a baseball cap, she'd loop around Castillo de San Marcos, along the shore of the Matanzas River, and over the Bridge of Lions. Turning around and coming back over the bridge, she'd ended at the Crucial Coffee hut for a brew before walking to her therapist's office. The Ancient City was thick with more than four hundred years of history that Lillian could rarely recall through memorized dates and facts. However, she always enjoyed the stories of the human struggle. She was entranced by stories of the towns-people retreating to the fort during pirate raids or the English sieges to protect their family's lives in the early settlements.

Joshua was always ready to give a lesson on the local history. The trolley bells and cannon fire from the Castillo provided a surround-sound soundtrack working synergistically with his words. The click, clack, click of the horse-drawn carriage provided the percussion, while the whish of sea breeze through the sailboat masts added the string section. He once stopped in his tracks, on a walk around the city, and pointed out to the water.

"Lil! The Matanzas River and inlet were named after the Spanish slaughter of French military shipwreck survivors at the mouth of that very inlet. About two hundred Frenchmen were massacred by Pedro Menendez and his men. In Spanish, Matanzas means 'slaughter' because the river sat red with blood that day," he explained. She was reminded of the Egyptian blood plague in Exodus, where just a strike of Aaron's staff had turned the water to blood, causing all the fish to die and making the water undrinkable. Lillian had been struck that the event was one of many examples of the miraculous power of God, revealed tangibly in front of people who saw it but remained unbelieving.

She would typically drink a bottle of water while waiting for her usual—a dirty, skinny, chai tea latte with almond milk and a dash of cinnamon. Sometimes she'd order it hot because she would feel cold when her sweat dried, and sometimes cold because the hot air, while enjoyable, could be brutal. She would walk swiftly west, down Cuna Street, until she approached Cordova Street. Then she'd turn left, and the two-story office building on the left, just past the Maple Street Biscuit Company, was where he'd be waiting for her.

Chapter 76

He never seemed to mind her sweat.

"You're welcome to always come as you are," her therapist had explained at their first session. She felt she needed to explain anyway and went into her diatribe that she needed to run in the morning before a busy day of clients, and the only time to fit her own therapy sessions in would be immediately after the run—before heading home to shower and get ready for the day. He nodded patiently as if he understood.

"I'm an early riser. These early appointments are the perfect time for me," he had offered.

Lillian immediately felt comfortable at her first intake session. He offered open body language and had a non-judgmental focus.

"Be aware, since I'm a therapist myself, we tend to be tough clients," she had warned him with a chuckle. He laughed with her.

"I'm up for the challenge," he reassured her. His smile was gentle and warm as he gestured towards a cozy-looking couch with two oversized pillows advertising "Beach Life" embroidered on one and "Saltwater Vibes" on the other. He had dark-brown eyes with hair to match. His skin was olive-toned and remarkably unblemished. The office colors were earthy and relaxing. It smelled of sweet incense. Lillian inhaled slow and deep and was sure she identified sweet pine and ginseng. On the center of a humble, wooden coffee table, stood a small, brown, clay vase, filled with white lilies.

"Also, since I'm a therapist and I do this every day, you can skip the disclaimers and explanations of the therapeutic relationship and all that," she reassured him. He gave a nod and another gentle smile.

"Got it. Thanks for that. What brings you to me?" he asked.

"So, I don't want to beat around the bush like those clients who take weeks and weeks before finally exposing their pain and getting to the heart of the matter. I'm just going to throw it all at you, okay? Ready? Put on your seat belt!" Lillian cautioned.

"Lay it all on me. I can handle it. I'm ready," he replied while visibly tightening an imaginary seatbelt. She continued.

"I'm a pastor's kid. I have always felt that my dad put more into the church than his own family. We are not close. I have no siblings—no sister to share and keep my secrets, no brother to defend me against bullies. My mom intentionally overdosed and died when I was fourteen, and shortly after that my best friend, my dog, drowned and I found him dead. When my mom was alive, she was self-absorbed, lost in her own thoughts, and when she left, she offered me no words of wisdom, no note, no bread-crumbs to help me move on. I loved a man when I was just a teenager, but he only saw me as a younger sister. He maintained good boundaries with me, but at the time, I felt rejected and unlovable. I lost my virginity to the baseball coach when I was in high school and then he dismissed me. I slept with my married youth pastor when I was eighteen, got pregnant, and had an abortion. He insisted I get rid of the problem and then abandoned me. Somehow, despite all that, I help people heal and I'm married to an incredible man, but I don't feel healed or worthy. I'm pregnant now and I haven't told my husband; I can't imagine I'd be a good mom. What if I end up like my mother?" They sat looking at each other for a moment when she finished, her therapist never breaking eye contact, like he could measure the depths of her soul.

"That is a lot of pain and loss, Lillian. I'm so sorry for those layers of hurt for you," he validated.

"Yeah, it is a lot. It's heavy," she had responded. She recalled at least four or five subsequent sessions of sharing thoughts, feelings, and perspectives. She shared every aspect of her life with him. She told him in detail her frustrations with God her Creator, man, and man-made religions. She made no apologies. It felt good to get it all out. But it was the last session that had brought out a physiological reaction and crucial paradigm shift in her.

Chapter 77

"Tell me more about your relationship with your earthly father, Lillian," he pushed her.

"I told you. We're not close," she replied.

"What does 'not close' look like?" he inquired.

"I never really felt accepted by him. We hardly hugged or cuddled. I didn't feel affirmed. He was so busy 'doing God's work' that he seemed to not notice that I needed work too. I should have come first. Especially after my mother took her own life. I told you, I might end up like her!"

"I hear you. I see you, Lillian. Tell me the ways you haven't ended up like your mother," he urged. Lillian swallowed hard.

"Well, when things were difficult or painful, I didn't quit. That's one thing." She continued, "When I feel sad or anxious, I fight, I try. I use my pain to help others heal. I have empathy and compassion." She paused. "And I will never be a mother, so I won't fail my child. I won't ruin them and allow them to feel alone and confused and then recklessly, violently abandon them." Heavy guilt surfaced as she thought about the abortion instrument recklessly and violently sucking and killing her previous child. Then she instinctively considered how she was planning to repeat the same violent process to this child! She began to breathe rapidly as she felt herself entering a panic attack. She sprang forward from the couch to her knees in front of her therapist, gasping and pressing her chest with her palm. He joined her on the floor.

"Lillian, child, breathe. Slow it down. In and out, slowly, in and out, with me now," he gently commanded her. He modeled the breathing he wanted her to mimic and spoke over her. "You're okay. You are safe. You are loved," he stated. They were the words she had spoken to so many clients over the years, providing them comfort, helping them through panic attacks. Now they were being spoken over her. He continued. "Lillian you are forgiven. You carry a very heavy cross every day and avoid Abba, who wants to hold you in His arms. Understand that you carry a cross that is not yours to carry. Your Savior chose to carry it and to be nailed to it for you as a gift. You have choices too. You have a second chance to make a different choice, to be a mother unlike yours, to break a dark cycle, to fulfill our Father's purpose for your life. You have a chance to allow your child to live a purposeful life." He spoke with authority and compassion. He sounded sincere and compelling. "Lillian, you seek affection, acceptance, and affirmation from broken people, in a broken world that ebbs and flows. Those mortal, human people will always fall short. But Your Father God has always felt this way about you. You can rest in Him." She was taken aback, shocked, and confused. He spoke with a heavenly mindset, not an earthly one. He sat with her while her breathing returned to normal. In unison they breathed, his hands on her shoulders, looking into her eyes, as if there were only one set of lungs in the room. Her tears fell like gentle rain. His long-sleeved shirt had ridden up on his arms where she suddenly noticed what appeared to be scars on the inner sides of his wrists. *He has known pain in his life, too.*

Chapter 78

It was after midnight, already Friday morning. Joshua had had a night-cap with Elijah after his last class and entered his quiet home, greeted by a tired Leo, who mustered enough strength to wag his tail. He smiled when he saw the lamp turned on by the front door. He recognized Lillian's instinct to leave Leo with a night light even though she left with plenty of daylight pouring into their home. Joshua knelt and rubbed as Leo rolled over on his back in surrender. His eyes moved toward piles of trash that were spread all over the kitchen floor, communicating how Leo felt about Mommy leaving him and Daddy coming home late.

"Leo! What have you done?" Joshua used his deepest stern voice to let Leo know how he, in turn, felt about his behavior. As he mentally prepared a lecture to admonish Leo's bad choice, his eyes narrowed in on an object that brought both elation and doom in a wave of conflicting emotions. He spotted a pregnancy stick with the word "pregnant" clearly displayed on the indicator window.

His mind raced through a mental checklist, a slow-motion picture book flipping in his head. Lillian had complained of sore breasts and blamed chafing from running. She had not touched their favorite wine over the past few weeks, claiming dehydration and headaches. She seemed distant and distracted, a lower libido, stuck in her own world, not allowing him in. He had not pushed her to talk. WHY had he not pushed her?

He had looked up her location on a phone app earlier and saw she was safe at their hotel in Coral Gables, when she had not responded to his texts or calls. He knew his wife often forgot to check her phone after putting it on silent, trying to decompress from the world. He looked for her laptop, not in its usual spot, and found it slid under the couch, barely sticking out.

"Password, password," he whispered. Trying two options without success, he finally got in on the third time. He immediately searched her history. Unfortunately, he found exactly what he was hoping he would not. He needed to act quickly. Not wanting to take the time to drop Leo anywhere, Joshua quickly stuffed a bag with essentials and headed back to the car with Leo trotting behind. Leo paused to empty his bladder on a nearby, grass-like muscari plant but hopped right in the car with Joshua's whistle.

He backed out of the drive and sped down the coastline, multitasking with several texts from the house and making several phone calls inside the car to Lillian, Elijah, and Hailey. Although she was tucked safely in her hotel bed right now, he knew where she was heading and what she was planning. He knew her heart and thoughts so well … His first emotions were regret and fear. He wished he had pushed her more to process her past, and he wished he had supported her more so she wouldn't let past decisions cloud her judgment or make her question her value.

Chapter 79

Talking to himself out loud, Joshua felt his tension building, as he realized the magnitude of the events that were unfolding before him. "I'm patient. Or at least I'm mostly patient. We've been circling around this issue for years and I thought we'd come to a sort of 'détente.' I can't believe she'd just steal away and do this so deceptively. Our situation is different this time! This baby was conceived in love, even if she's not sure she's ready. This is so unfair. I give this stubborn, ungrateful woman my whole heart, my love, my empathy. I don't deserve this reaction! God, help me!" Joshua called out. Hearing his own voice in total distress startled him and then gave him pause. Immediately, he realized that Lillian would regret this. Not just the act itself, but the way she was doing it. He needed to separate his anger and frustration from the equation so he could help, not hurt.

"Father, please help me. I can't think enough to know what to say. Please intercede. I want so desperately for You to stop my wife from doing what I think she is doing. You know she's frightened and confused. Help me get to her in time, maybe put an obstacle in her way! I trust You, Lord! Just help her! Help us! In Jesus' name." Joshua spoke out loud in desperation.

After several hours, and with less than two hours to go, Joshua saw an array of red brake lights in front of him as he entered Broward County. Blinding yellow headlights on the northbound highway had traffic screeching to a complete stop. He reluctantly took his right foot off the gas pedal and pumped the brakes.

"No, no, no!" he wailed from the bottom of his chest cavity. In the middle of the highway, he saw an oil tanker upside down, surrounded by multiple fire trucks and ambulances. His eyes darted to the tree line, irrationally contemplating an off-road path that would get him around the roadblock and back on the path to his wife.

"God, I suggested an obstacle in my wife's way, not mine!" he lamented. His head dropped to the steering wheel for a second before he moved to park his car on the side of the road and cracked the window.

"Stay! I'll be right back." He pointed at Leo in the passenger seat and took off running ahead to a police officer.

"Excuse me, sir, you need to get back into your car. We have a Life Flight chopper inbound and it's going to land in this area any moment now," the highway patrol officer explained while he held out his hand. "We've got multiple casualties, including young children." Joshua was horrified, nodding his head in understanding.

"Oh God! That's horrible!" It made him think of his own child and the danger he or she was also in. He paused, feeling the conflict inside his heart grow. He started to turn to head back to Leo but only got a few steps. "But...officer, I hate to be that guy...but I can't help it. I'm going to have my own casualty to deal with if you won't help me through this jam. Please, I have to get to my wife in Coral Gables before morning. She needs me. It's really a matter of life and death also!" he pleaded.

The police officer's large cross tattoo on his bulging right bicep, with the word "*saved*" etched in it, caught his eye like a sign of hope. Joshua pointed at the tattoo.

"Please, my brother in Christ. I don't have any right to ask. And you don't have any obligation to help me. But is there any way...any way you can help me get to the other side of this?" he begged. It took several minutes, actually closer to an hour, but the officer asked another officer to cover his post as he worked with people to move their vehicles.

He turned to Joshua and said, "Follow me!" He put his siren on and cleared a path for Joshua through the sea of metal. Escorting him to an open highway, his last statement to Joshua resonated in his heart and caused goosebumps.

"I've been in a few situations before where a brother has helped me, and I feel the Holy Spirit convicting me to help you. I will pray for you—Godspeed."

Chapter 80

Unaware of the harrowing traffic accident that Joshua had navigated to reach her, Lillian awoke at the clinic to the reassurance of her husband's sweet, gentle voice.

"Lil, sweetheart, it's okay. I'm here," he murmured. Confused and assuming the procedure was over, she was instantly consumed with regret and wailed. Suddenly she was struck by how certain she was that she did not want to do it anymore. She clutched the front of Joshua's shirt tightly and aggressively with both fists, sending two buttons flying under the strain. She pleaded with him to forgive her and told him that she was sorry. She kept babbling and crying, too distraught to know what else to offer.

"You're okay. Our baby is okay. You just fainted in the hallway. They didn't move forward with the procedure because they had to make sure you were okay," Joshua replied. Relief was replaced by confusion as she wondered how he could possibly have found her. Did she leave clues? She was overwhelmed with emotions but devoid of words. She felt the need to explain—why she was there, what her memories of her client therapy sessions had come to mean to her. The flashbacks had initially been annoying, then exhausting, then intriguing. Now she had some bizarre clarity that the very separate lives of those individual clients were all interconnected on a spiritual level meant to teach her something.

"I didn't mean to deceive you, Joshua. Well, that's not true. I was just so compromised with my own thinking that I convinced myself I had no choice. I can't believe I'm here again. Our precious baby. I'm so sorry." Lillian pleaded for understanding and covered her face with her hands.

Joshua chose to embrace his wife. Gratitude gave him the ability to forgive. His heart filled with more love and tenderness for her than he ever believed possible. He nodded to the nurse, and she looked pointedly at Lillian.

"We're taking our baby home with us," Lillian said with great resolve. "There won't be a procedure for me today." Joshua sat Lillian down in a chair in the hallway while he stood at the counter, signing her discharge paperwork. Down the hallway, a fleeting movement caught her eye. Lillian strained forward to see, still regaining all her faculties after fainting. She caught a quick glance of a man she thought she recognized. *What? It couldn't be. It really looked like her therapist, but he lived in St. Augustine. What would he be doing in Coral Gables?* She dismissed the thought as the double doors shut, thinking to herself, *wow, I'm still so rattled!*

Lillian and Joshua left the clinic and went back to her hotel room to ride out the storm together. Leo greeted them exuberantly as they entered the room.

"I had to leave so fast—I brought him with. I told Maria at the front desk that I forgot my key and needed something from our room. Then I snuck him in the back exit," Joshua explained. Lillian, beyond grateful to have the loving greeting of her fur baby, fell to her knees and engulfed him with scratches and kisses.

"Who's a good boy, sneaking in hotel rooms with Daddy?" she teased, the tension finally starting to drain from her body.

"I must not be good at sneaking though; shortly after I brought him in, Maria was at the door smiling at me with two dog bowls in hand. She told me to let her know if I needed anything else and winked at me. She reminded me that this is a pet-friendly hotel," Joshua explained sheepishly.

Thunder crashed in the distance and they both glanced at the window. It was the beginning of the storm's outer bands. Lillian considered that the possible destructive storm that was approaching would be nothing compared to the internal storm she had been battling for many years. With hurricane snacks and plenty of bottled water stocked from the front desk, they were ready for anything the night brought. Depleted, Lillian shed her clothing down to a tank top and underwear and crawled under the bedsheets. It wasn't even noon, but the mental exhaustion of reliving therapy sessions combined with the weight of her secret had her feeling like she just conquered the entirety of Mount Kilimanjaro all in a day.

Chapter 81

Joshua joined her, spooning, with Lillian as the little spoon, as he snuggled in close to her. His presence and protective embrace grounded her and offered the safety she needed to begin drifting off to sleep.

"Joshua," she said wearily, "I feel so heavy with remorse because of what I did all those years ago and almost did again, but now so relieved and I want to help women who feel trapped now or unworthy because of their past." Lillian yawned. "I feel driven to help other women like me who might feel scared or confused," she murmured urgently.

"An unbeliever may not understand because they don't see through spiritual eyes. But what you've experienced is called a transformation; it's called being forgiven, my love. It's the very foundation of our faith. It's the mighty power of the Holy Spirit in you." Joshua declared.

"Yes! And who better to advocate for other women than me? Someone who went through what I did? I remember the story of Saul who persecuted Christians, then transformed on the road to Damascus. He is later called Paul and subsequently becomes one of the greatest evangelists for Christ!" Lillian affirmed. She was drained from the roller coaster of thoughts and emotions over the past few weeks.

"I love you," they whispered simultaneously as she began to give in to the pull of sleep. Joshua kissed his wife's head and breathed deep, smelling the sweet aroma of her hair. She began to snore.

The storm never fully hit the Florida shores. It skirted the coastline and turned by 3 a.m. It was as if the strong and intentional breath of God blew it away, commanding the elements with *not today ... not this time.*

While Joshua sat watching the gentle rain and wind cleanse the pool deck outside their window, Lillian started to wake up. The soft caresses of her husband drifted up and down her back and hips, causing her to sigh. He gently but intentionally rolled her over to face him and with a passionate, deep kiss, asked her how he could please her. Not waiting for instructions, his kisses moved to her breasts as his right hand explored the wetness emerging between her legs.

"That's a good start, baby," Lillian whispered through the pleasure. She pulled his boxers down and helped him enter her, a perfect fit. They became one. With each thrust, Joshua looked deep into his wife's eyes.

"I love you!" he implored.

"I love you too, so much!" she managed to respond through gasps for air between moans. They pleasured each other the way God intended it to be in a consensual, committed relationship. Two servants, each putting the other first, and by doing so, each one finding unexplainable bliss.

Afterwards, wrapped in a blanket, Lillian walked towards the sliding glass door to watch the rain. Joshua followed and stopped behind her. She impulsively stepped outside into the rainwater, imagining a physical cleansing to match the spiritual and emotional one she felt she'd just experienced. She observed Joshua search the sky for lightning before joining her. He held her face in his hands and kissed the rainwater as it fell and rolled down her cheeks. Leo joined them for his own shower and lifted his leg near the patio gate.

Chapter 82

"Hurricanes, tornados, earthquakes, pandemics, and fires are all signs of the earth ebbing and flowing, cracking, erupting, and longing for its Creator, just as we humans do," Lillian shared her insight about storms humans face on Earth to her husband. "Even non-believers long for 'something' or 'someone' beyond themselves. All mankind longs for acceptance, affection, and affirmation, Joshua! These desires, combined with the imperfect, sinful nature of humans, produce trauma and brokenness that can lead to substance abuse, dysfunctional relationship cycles, bullying, racism, rape, abortion, adultery, personality and eating disorders, gossip, persecution, war and so much more. So, we have a world full of people focused on themselves who are unable to live up to their heart's desires, within their own flesh. We place faith in man-made religion, run by imperfect people, who will eventually let you down in some way or another. Our faith should be in the loving Father, who will never let you down. Ours is a broken earth where the enemy, the prince of this temporary world, the father of lies, Satan, capitalizes on all of this. It further plants seeds of doubt, fear, and anxiety, and round and round we go," Lillian said breathlessly, warming to her subject.

"Joshua!" she urged as she ran back into the room so quickly, she startled Leo, who barked harshly, as he was already burrowing under a dry, fuzzy blanket on the floor. She opened the nightstand drawer and grabbed the Holy Bible. She could have searched on her phone, but something about the moment made her feel she needed to get back to the basics and hold the book in her hands that she had dismissed a lot over the years. She flipped to the book of Matthew, mumbling as she searched.

"Where is it? Where is it? Aha! Joshua, in Matthew 3:17, Matthew 17:5, and 2 Peter 1:17, per the cross reference, God says to Jesus, 'This is my son, whom I love; with him I am well pleased.' This applies to us as children of God when we accept Jesus as the Son of God, as our Savior. This is God saying to us, 'This is my son, daughter, beloved, child, loved one.' This is the acceptance that everyone longs for—those who come from broken homes, absent or abusive parents, foster children. 'Whom I love,' it says. That is the affection that everyone longs for: abuse survivors, neglected or abandoned people, absent parents, broken relationships. 'With him, her, they, them, I am well-pleased.' That is the affirmation for which everyone longs. Harsh and rejecting parents, coaches, teachers, bosses, neglectful caregivers, bullies, those with regret, shame, or guilt. Those are all words from the mouth of God to His Son, His Son who lives in every one of us if we ask Him. The key to peace, joy, love, and hope is not self-acceptance or man's acceptance. Humans will always fall short. It's Christ's acceptance, the Christ who is in us! Therefore, we are all fully accepted, loved, and affirmed by the Father God!" Lillian began to sob. "I get it, Joshua. I finally get it. I had flashback memories of specific clients all day yesterday and this morning, buzzing in my head, one after another! But out of all the clients that I've counseled over the years, and many who never found closure or healing, my flashbacks were only of a specific few who had a foundation of faith. And I'm thinking, why? I never advertised myself as a Christian counselor. 'Christian' isn't even an adjective, it's a noun. I never wanted to limit myself to just people of faith; I wanted to help all people. Then I had vivid recollections of my own therapy sessions with my therapist. And he spoke some hard truths to me, Joshua! Let me tell you, like, he looked into my soul! Then all the session memories seemed to come together and point me to the ultimate truth and only source of joy. It's all about what Jesus did!" she proclaimed.

"Yes, sweetheart, I couldn't have articulated that any better. So beautiful! But what do you mean, your own therapy sessions? I didn't know you were going to therapy," Joshua questioned.

"I've had a few sessions in the past several weeks, in the early mornings, after my runs, before I started seeing clients. The office is the terracotta two-story, two-toned building on Cordova Street, with the Spanish tile roof. You know the one," she probed. Joshua sat and pondered. His thinking wrinkle emerged on his forehead. Clearly, the idea of another secret produced a pained look of regret on his face.

"Lil, that building has been for rent or sale for ages. Are you sure it was that one?" he questioned. She bristled, slightly irritated.

"Yes, Joshua, I think I know what building I walked to for therapy," she said, raising an eyebrow.

Lillian went on to explain and reiterate how the day she left on her trip, out of her hundreds of clients over the past several years, it seemed God was flooding her mind with specific clients. What they seemed to have in common was that all, at some point in their lives, were believers and that each and every one had to surrender to God's truth to find healing. It was as if God was reminding her of her own struggles saying, *Surrender to me, Lil.*

"Thank you, God! I think I've fallen deeper in love with you, if that's even possible," Joshua whispered and cried with her.

Chapter 83

When the sun rose that Saturday morning, they drove back north, following each other home to Saint Augustine. Heavy traffic flow was heading back south. She wished they could ship one car home and ride together. After what they had been through, she just needed more time. She had thought about leaving one car at her dad's house, as they stood in the hotel parking lot getting ready to trek back. Joshua offered to fly down the following Friday and drive it back. Lillian considered it for a moment but decided against it.

"I don't want you to have to do that. It's kind of my mess we are having to clean up and I shouldn't hand off the inconvenient and difficult stuff. I need you to know I just don't want to be apart. I don't ever want to separate again," she clarified. Joshua held her hands and pulled her into him, kissing her tenderly. He was not normally a fan of public displays of affection, but in the moment, he must have changed his mind. He agreed that they would not go out of town without the other ever again, if possible. They drove closely, one behind the other the whole trip. They stopped for gas together and took bathroom breaks, taking turns walking Leo on the grass areas.

While driving, Lillian reflected on how the idea of heading "home" had a different meaning to her now than it had previously. It would no longer feel like a house full of ghosts in the nursery. The halls would illuminate with her angels instead. Lillian would use another one of her favorite therapy techniques for herself now. She enjoyed helping young parents write about and process the traumatic relationships in their past, exorcising their "ghosts," and then directing them to recognize their "angels." Those who came along in their lives and showed a glimpse of love, compassion, or kindness were true angels. Focusing on the angels is what moved people beyond their haunted pasts.

Often, focusing on the ghosts prevented caregivers from forming healthy bonds with their infants and, subsequently, the infants don't form healthy attachments. These bonds and attachments are needed for baby brains to create and grow as many neuron connections as possible. Every touch, rub, kiss, and interaction results in critical nerve cells sending messages. When a client was unable to remember or recognize an angel initially, during therapy, Lillian helped by being a safe person who provided empathy and hope. Some people came to her so consumed in the storms of their life that they couldn't see the rainbows, much less the angels. Sometimes it would take several sessions before a client would remember, *oh, yeah, I had a third-grade teacher who was always nice to me and saw my potential;* or *I had a coach who took the time to notice my strengths and pushed me to be my best.*

Lillian took that quiet driving time to reflect on her own angels. She thought about her maternal preschool teacher who taught her how to blow the butterflies out of her stomach, and her quiet, strong, consistent grandfather. She remembered Dean, her first and second gentle kiss, no strings attached. She smiled with memories of Jeremiah, the man who constantly rescued her from injuries when she was thirteen and fourteen, never expecting anything in return. He had always seen the fragile and injured teenage girl who needed someone to return her to outdoor adventures a little bit wiser and more cautious. She could see now that he removed himself from her life's path so she could grow. As long as he remained present, she would have been stuck in a state of idolizing him. She remembered Dr. Suarez, who saw something special in her and encouraged her to rise to her fullest potential academically and professionally. There were many professors and supervisors who spurred her on along the way. Also, there were her aunt and uncle, who took her in and helped her endure the loss of her beloved Benji with patience and gentle words. She thought of her father. If she removed the anger and frustration she held against him, he was an angel in her nursery too. He had never abandoned her; he was always there.

Maybe he wasn't always saying or doing the right thing, but she sure didn't make it easy on him, and as she grew and matured, she never told him what she needed from him.

Then there was Joshua, the man God set aside for her who would lead her back to Him with his enduring love and mercy. She couldn't forget her therapist, who listened intently, non-judgmentally, and seemed to breath her into emotional healing. Above all, there was Jesus. He endured pain and suffering He did not deserve so that Lillian, and every other believer who deserved death, could be reconciled with Abba in eternal paradise. He offered the promise of a new Earth, a new Heaven, and perfect Heavenly bodies to come. That alone should be enough, Lillian admitted. But the human ailment would always make us think and feel we wanted and needed more, as we lived in broken, temporary bodies on a broken, temporary earth.

Chapter 84

The evacuators drove back south, opposite of Lillian and Joshua, relieved they had homes to go back to, she was sure. They still had time to pack their coolers, gas up their boats, fire up their grills, and enjoy their weekend before business-as-usual reconvened Monday morning. Lillian hoped the family by the pool was making their way back to the Keys for more family memories. Leo sat as Lillian's co-pilot, tail wagging and tongue hanging, without a care in the world. He was oblivious to another five-plus-hour car ride. He was just happy to be in the presence of his mommy with check-ins to see daddy. Joshua insisted she drive ahead so he could keep his eyes on her. He had expressed an equal need to lead and protect her, so they agreed he would follow behind.

The atmosphere in the car felt remarkably simple and light. The heaviness she'd driven down with had evaporated. Lillian felt nothing but joy and acceptance. Her cognitive dissonance washed away. Her thoughts and feelings realigned. There was no condemnation or judgment from Joshua, God, or herself. *There was no such thing as a punishing God,* she reminded herself. Humans punish themselves and each other, projecting our dysfunction as God's wrath. The Holy Spirit catches every tear and grieves with us. She imagined God saying, *Look at me! I am here. I am madly in love with you. I am for you. My Son died for you. Stop comparing me to earthly relationships that fail you!*

Leo welcomed his yard and home with a wagging tail, to and fro, painting affirmations in the air as he trotted ahead. He galloped straight to his favorite queen palm and lifted his leg. Unloading bags and entering through the kitchen, the trash still lay all over the tiled floor. Joshua had left with Leo in such a hurry, he didn't have time to clean up; he had become hyper focused on finding his wife. But looking down at the pile with Lillian standing beside him, he pulled from the pile the positive pregnancy test she had used the morning she left to verify one more time and smiled. He was going to be a father. By the grace of God, he would be a father. The reality was just starting to sink in, she could tell.

"That was my third test, Joshua. I prayed this one would be negative as a reprieve from my biggest fear. I'm so thankful God didn't answer this prayer. I understand now that when our prayers aren't answered how we want, it's because of His infinite wisdom. He always knows what's best," Lillian explained. Joshua looked at his wife adoringly.

Leo seemed to notice the mess on the floor and, perhaps remembering he did it, offered a whine and slunk under the kitchen table, looking guilty. Waiting for his consequence, Lillian had to crawl under the table to meet Leo where he was at and hug him.

"You're not in trouble, boy. You helped Daddy save Mommy. You helped Mommy be rescued. Good came out of your bad choice to break into the trash," she explained and reassured him. Leo slowly began wagging his tail, accepting his mommy's love and approval. He rolled over on his back and fully submitted, his go-to move. As she rubbed his belly, Lillian had another realization that it was very much the way our relationship is with God. He sees the messes we make, meets us where we are at, loves us unconditionally, and uses it for good. That had been another reoccurring theme in her client flashbacks over the past few days. It was also a theme in her own life. Her father's continual childhood line came to her head again.

"Choose to wear the crown of beauty, Lil; let God wipe away your ashes," he'd declared. That statement used to make her so angry she wanted to spit, but now with a softened heart, she found meaning in it.

She understood that, as a believer, when you seek a relationship with God through Jesus, you no longer need to mourn, be disgraced, or be ashamed of your past mistakes because they do not define you. To her, the ashes represented mourning, and the crown of beauty represented redemption, which should provide joy. Moving forward, Lillian would choose joy.

Chapter 85

S unday brought sunshine and the smell of coffee, bacon, and omelets. Now that she was living in the open, fully accepting the life growing inside her, her body was bombarded with the symptoms of full-on morning sickness. She ended up drinking a half glass of orange juice and making a taco, the only thing that satisfied her nausea.

"This pregnancy food journey is going to be fun!" Joshua declared while laughing. The church bells across the street that tended to bring a pang of disappointment for Lillian were now a welcoming sound and a reminder of the harmony God can bring to your soul when you surrender to Him.

Joshua suggested home church. Finding their way back into bed, Leo demanded his place in the middle as they enjoyed worship music and listened to a sermon streaming online from a local non-denominational church. Joshua held tight to Lillian's hand, with his other hand placed gently on her stomach. He closed his eyes and prayed specifically, the way his mother had taught him, using the Lord's Prayer as a template.

"Dear Father God, You are an awesome God, the Most High, our Creator! We ask Your will be done in our lives. Forgive our sins in our hearts, minds, and actions. Father, shut the mouths of our enemies and soften their hearts so they may know you. Thank you for this beautiful day and for always providing for our needs. Thank you for my wife and the precious life growing inside of her. Thank you for entrusting us to be parents. Thank you for eternal life given by the sacrifice of your Son, Jesus. Protect us from the evil one, Lord, and may none of his schemes penetrate our lives. May no weapon formed against us stand. We give you all the praise and glory. In Jesus' name, Amen." Joshua looked up the verse of the day on his Bible app and smiled.

"Wow, how appropriate, Lil. Remember when you read this, that there are no coincidences when you are a believer! Read this verse as if God is reading it personally to you. Put your name in it," he prompted Lillian while handing her his phone.

"Proverbs 31:28, [Lillian's] children arise and call her blessed; her husband, [Joshua] also, and he praises her.'" Lillian read it out loud and her eyes filled with tears that ran down her cheeks and into her mouth; the salty taste was welcomed. It would be the second time in two days that she'd cried tears of joy, after years of sorrow.

They both agreed to take a walk to the building where Lillian insisted she'd had numerous therapy sessions. Before leaving, Joshua rolled onto his right side and, using his right arm and hand as a kickstand to hold his head up, he leaned into his wife.

"Before we go, I have a question," he declared while he kissed her forehead, her cheek, her nose, her lips, and her chin, navigating his way around her face with tenderness and authority.

"Ask me anything, just don't stop kissing me," she teased.

"Are you keeping anything else from me? We can't have secrets, sweetheart. Are there any undisclosed areas of your heart that you would be willing to share with me? I don't want the enemy to have a foothold. Secrets between spouses become the devil's playground. I'm your husband and I love all of you, past, present, and future. We are supposed to be one, Lil. I need you to give me your whole heart," he implored.

Lillian remembered her thoughts about Jeremiah the days before, how she realized that she had held back a piece of her heart from her husband. She had realized that as long as she held on to that part of her past and allowed Jeremiah to retain residence there, she was not fully her husband's.

"There is a part of my past that I never told you about, that I've been keeping to myself. I realize you deserve to know, and I need to let it go," she explained. Joshua kissed her again, making direct eye contact, and waited patiently.

"Tell me, sweetheart," he encouraged.

Chapter 86

She began her recollections of the North and her first memories of Jeremiah. She explained that he was seven years older than her and entered her life when she was in middle school, specifically the summer before and after eighth grade. She related how he always rescued her when she injured herself, loved her like a little sister, played catch with her, listened, and talked to her, but she had romantic feelings for him.

She further explained that she fantasized that he would wait for her, and when she was eighteen, he would swoop in and marry her. Then she related how devastating it was when he attended her mother's funeral, gave her a bracelet, and walked away from her for good. After that, she described how losing her bracelet, never to be found at the bottom of the lagoon, was more devastation. She recalled the Bible verse etched in the bracelet, 1 Peter 5:10, that she never looked up, out of protest for everything God had taken away from her. She shared the nuggets of hope and love Jeremiah offered her about forgiving her enemies and remembering that God had a plan for her life—that she was beloved.

She cried and laughed throughout her storytelling. Joshua listened intently, holding her left hand in his and kissing it every so often. He smiled when she smiled. He wiped tears when she cried. She shared everything she could remember. It was cathartic and, just as she thought, by speaking it into the air, she felt her heart release the childhood fantasy. The act of surrender allowed more room for her husband. When she was finished, she stared at Joshua.

"I'm so glad you had him. I'm so thankful he was a good and kind man in your life," Joshua replied, grabbing his physical Bible next to their bed on the nightstand. He looked up 1 Peter 5:10 and read it out loud to Lillian, placing her name in the scripture.

"And the God of all grace, who called [Lillian] to his eternal glory in Christ, after [Lillian] has suffered a little while, will himself restore [her] and make [her] strong, firm and steadfast." He spoke with passion. She was stunned. A verse picked out for her by Jeremiah when she was fourteen years old proved to encapsulate her life's mantra thus far. She looked forward to the restoration and strength that verse promised.

Chapter 81

After lunch, Lillian, hand in hand with Joshua, took a short walk a few blocks north, to show him her therapist's office. She knew he probably wouldn't be there on a Sunday, and it was inappropriate to show up without an appointment. However, she thought if she could see his name on the door and prove to Joshua where she had been going, she would feel more settled.

They approached the building. The terracotta colors from her memories, now that they stood in front of it, were more of a mauve with red licorice shutters around the windows. The front door looked like a delicious chocolate Hershey bar. The real estate sign hung like an out-of-place billboard and brought the return of a butterfly or two back to life in Lillian's stomach. She took a long, deep breath in and out through her nose and called the number displayed. Putting her phone on speaker so Joshua could hear, she waited. She knew real estate agents worked on Sundays and hoped someone would answer.

"Good afternoon, thank you for calling the real estate office of Donna Lonna; what kind of property do you think you wanna?" a gentle, soft-spoken, older female voice replied with a Southern twang, like Aunt Clara's. Lillian laughed after hearing the fun rhyme roll out in such a poetic way. The voice in her head begged, *can you please be my mom? You sound so fun!* Lillian was reminded of the need to laugh and how laughter had been lacking in her life lately.

"Hello, I'm inquiring about the property for rent and/or sale on Cordova Street. Can you tell me how long this property has been vacant?" Lillian questioned. The sweet woman continued to serenade Lillian, giving her a full history, including the current rental rate and a follow-up of three different times she would be happy to meet her at the property for a tour that week.

Lillian felt a foggy haze of astonishment and confusion surround her as she clenched Joshua's arm. He escorted her to sit down on a bench nearby. Despite the heat, chills ran up her spine and goosebumps appeared on her arms. She and Joshua looked at each other like a couple of deer caught in the headlights. She hadn't heard much of what was said after Donna Lonna had informed her that it had been vacant for about fourteen months.

"To clarify, no one has rented any space on this property in the last fourteen months?" Lillian was able to articulate one more question.

"That's right, honey. I mean, I am ready to give this place away at this point. Oh, dear, I didn't mean that. I can't just give it away. Would you like to see it?" Donna Lonna corrected.

"Yes, yes, I am interested. I will call you back soon," Lillian confirmed. She hung up the phone and they headed back home, both agreeing to call Lillian's father and share the revelation with him. Her father was heavy in her thoughts. She didn't know why, but she felt an overwhelming desire to call him. Elijah and Hailey's words were in her head too: *When things don't make sense, consider the spiritual.*

Their trek home was much faster, and they both agreed that with a baby on the way, she should consider moving her counseling sessions away from their home property. Their detached cottage could become a playhouse or an art studio. Either way, they'd figure it out. But that could be set aside for a more pressing matter.

"Joshua, I'm confused; this doesn't make sense. I know this is the building where I came to see him," Lillian emphasized. As they walked, Lillian looked in her phone contacts for a saved phone number … nothing. She searched for a business card in her pocket cardholder … nothing.

Chapter 88

Knowing that Leo was ready for playtime but needing to make one more important phone call without distractions, Lillian and Joshua avoided the main house and snuck into her detached cottage along the privacy hedge, where Leo could not see them through the windows. It was as if they were teenagers sneaking into their tree fort for a kiss, under their parents' radar. Feeling overheated and slightly dizzy, she retrieved a coconut water out of her minifridge, sat down in her office chair, and called her dad. Her hands were shaking.

"It's okay, I'm here. You're not alone," Joshua sat close and reassured her.

"Lillian? I was just about to call you," her dad answered, with a shaky voice to match her shaky hands. She had a moment of guilt that they had been in Coral Gables for a few days and had not reached out to him. She started with small talk.

"Hey, Dad, I have you on speaker. Joshua is here too. I was going to make sure you were okay with the hurricane and all, but I saw that it had turned away from the coast," she rationalized.

"Hello, Joshua! Oh, you know me … even if it hadn't, I was buckled down and ready for what fury it brought. God is our protector," he asserted. Then his voice became serious. "Lillian, I was about to call you because I had a dream last night." Lillian listened intently. He continued, "I was in the throne room of God just like in the book of Revelation, Chapter 1, verse 17. Except it wasn't John, it was me. I fell at the feet of Jesus, as though I was dead. He placed His right hand on me and said, 'Do not be afraid. I am the living One. Now hear my words.'" He paused. Lillian listened intently.

"Dad? Are you still there?" she inquired. He cleared his throat.

"Yes, I'm sorry, I'm, I'm overwhelmed," he explained.

"What were His words?" she pressed.

"He gently rebuked me for denying your needs after the accident, I mean, your mother's suicide. I am so sorry, Lillian, that I was not there for you to talk about it when you needed me. I avoided the conversation to avoid the pain. I couldn't accept that she would take her own life and leave us. Then you lost Benji. I took you away from your childhood home and your summer friends so we could start over. By denying it and burying it, I was ignoring your pain. In my whole life, I will never understand what that did to you. You did so well in high school, in life, and you have had so many accomplishments. I rationalized that they were proof you were fine and strong, instead of looking deeper to really see. I understand now that you may have been quietly suffering, forced to wear a mask, forced to question your faith. I'm so sorry, Lillian, please forgive me," he urged.

Lillian, initially taken back, not used to showing any type of emotion in front of her dad except little explosions of anger throughout the years, allowed her deep-seated sadness to surface and reveal itself through the flow of tears and sobs.

"Dad," was all she managed.

"Mr. Michaelson, she needs a minute," Joshua jumped in, clearing his throat.

Lillian worked to collect herself. She struggled to adjust to the constant flow of emotions, partly because of the pregnancy hormones, no doubt, but also because of her opened heart, made tender by the work of the Holy Spirit. Lillian forgave her father and asked for forgiveness in return. There was no need to hash anything out. *I'm sorry and I forgive you* cancelled everything on both ends. Lillian realized that this was the power of the Holy Spirit when believers reconciled.

"I'm pregnant, Dad. I'm going to be a mom. You're going to be a grandpa. If you ever can consider moving close by, I know a real estate agent who could help," she offered her news with elation.

Lillian went on to explain the confusing memories of her own therapy sessions, followed by the discovery that there was no trace of her therapist.

She shared the fact that she had memories of her therapist just before she felt lightheaded and then fainted. Joshua shared his perspective and filled in some of the gaps, while Lillian sat listening in shock and awe. They left out the part about the clinic. Her father didn't need to hear all her truth. He did not need to pick up and carry the burden of the past that she had finally let go of. That was between her, her husband, and God.

"*It was a miracle. It was God revealing Himself to you! He pursued you,*" her father declared.

Chapter 89

J oshua took his wife's hand and led her to their bicycles. He placed Leo in her bicycle basket as he told her they had one more thing they needed to do that day. They rode through the streets, taking shortcuts only locals would know. He told her to trust him and follow along as he led her to a flower shop on San Marco Avenue.

"Be right back," Joshua reassured her as he left his bike near the window. Lillian pulled up beside him, accepted his quick kiss, and waited.

"What's Daddy up to, buddy? He knows I don't like flowers. It's so sad when they die," she asserted softly, while scratching Leo's head.

Joshua exited the store with a small bouquet of white lilies. He gently placed them in his bicycle basket and again prompted his wife to trust and follow him. They rode onto the property of Our Lady of La Leche National Shrine at Mission Nobre de Dios. They stowed their bikes, walked across the small bridge, and entered the heart of the grounds. Joshua explained that he knew how she felt about the Catholic Church and its rules, but it was the only grounds that led to the water, which featured a huge, stainless-steel cross. After all, he also explained that he knew that she loved many aspects of all the different denominations of Christianity, and now she had realized it was imperfect man that eroded the beauty of traditions and spirituality, never God.

"I thought of the best way to give you closure, for the loss of your baby when you were eighteen. You had no one supporting you, no one you could tell or talk to about it. You weren't valued by the people in your life. You were used and abandoned by a man of God. We almost lost our baby because you had not forgiven yourself for the past. I thought we could give it to God, once and for all, we could lay it at the foot of the cross together. We will acknowledge God's forgiveness, sweetheart. Move forward, restored," Joshua clarified, with tears forming. His heart and spirit seemed to hurt for his wife.

"I chose white lilies because they are supposed to be a symbol of the innocence restored to the soul of the departed. I want you to hold on to the knowledge that you will meet your child one day, on the other side of eternity. I thought we could pray, and you could throw the lilies into the water. You don't have to watch these flowers die in a vase at home. You can watch them float forward with the hope of God's promises," he gently explained.

Lillian slumped down onto the bench behind them. The memories and guilt were like a weight, yet again, that physically drew her down. Joshua put his arms around his wife and hoisted her up.

"Lillian, speak to Abba," Joshua instructed.

She couldn't argue, her need for relief was so great. "God, please forgive me for not fighting for my baby many years ago," Lillian said, desperately choking for air. It was that simple. One sentence spoken from her heart and the weight was lifted. It didn't need to be spoken to a priest. It did not warrant a scarlet "A" to be branded on her for the remainder of her days. She gave a strong underarm throw, landing the lilies into the canal leading to the river. She nestled into her husband's arms, and they watched in silence as her shame and grief floated away. Leo ran to edge of the grass and barked; giving his own good-bye.

"Lil, when I was on my way to you, I prayed that God would put an obstacle in your way, to stop you. Then when I was delayed by a serious accident, I was so angry. Now I realize that my obstacle allowed God to intervene with you directly. I see how sometimes we need to get out of people's way and let Abba work. I'm your partner, but I know I can't and shouldn't be your everything. Only God can fulfill that role," Joshua shared. Lillian nodded in agreement. She understood that now, more than ever.

"Joshua, I realize too, as your wife, that you have carried my heavy burdens for so long and God wants us to have an equal partnership. Thank you for your patience, baby. I want to step it up and feed into your spiritual life just as much as you have fed into mine. We need to balance out our marriage," she announced. Joshua nodded. They held hands and watched until they couldn't see the lilies any longer.

Chapter 90

Laying in the backyard hammock that evening, Leo nestled closely, Lillian used her foot, hanging over one side, to barely rock them. She was battling mild nausea, maintained only by small nibbles of her salty crackers. Every time she took a bite, Leo opened one eye, waiting to see if he would get a taste of what he perceived as their shared treat. She was processing the weekend's events and trying to make sense of what Joshua and her father labeled as a miracle. She was mindful of the unexplainable joy that made her feel light and giddy.

The sky was painted pink with pops of orange and air-brushed purple, as the sun was slowly moving into slumber—as if nature was taking its time, indulging in its own beauty. With the French doors open, she could hear a podcast on fatherhood coming from the kitchen, combined with sounds of chopping and clanging. Joshua was making one of their favorite Mexican dishes called Topopo Salad to satisfy her cravings. *Topopo* literally translated meant 'volcano.' Not only was it delicious to eat, but the finished product was beautiful to look at. It was served in the shape of a volcano, sitting majestically on the plate, layers of chips, cheese, and lettuce reaching as high as gravity would allow. The drips of salsa represented lava and the black olives were rocks. They would switch up their choice of protein. Tonight's creation would include pulled chicken. It was an art activity just as much as it was a meal. It paired perfectly with her favorite sweet red wine, but Lillian's choice of drinks for the next year or so would only include water, juice, and milk.

They awaited the arrival of Elijah and Hailey, their brother and sister in Christ, on their way over for dinner. They had so much to tell them! They couldn't wait to tell them they were pregnant and ask them to be godparents. Joshua informed Lillian that Elijah and Hailey were coming over with their own news. It seemed that it would be an evening of intimate revelations. You could feel the anticipation in the air.

Laying with one hand on her belly, she took deep breaths in and out, in and out.

"I will make mistakes, but I will love you and put you first. I won't be perfect, but I will be better than my mother before me. I will fight for you, and, above all, you will know Jesus, little one," she whispered a promise to her unborn child. She closed her eyes and allowed her mind to slowly and fully open to endless possibilities. A montage of thoughts and events flooded her brain with an understanding that surpassed logic. Lillian's earth was shaken, and her thick, stubborn veil was finally aggressively torn as she realized with full clarity that the man, she had seen at the clinic that day *was* indeed her therapist, but she had never actually gone to therapy.

She saw him as clear as a sweet summer's day in the clinic, his unblemished olive skin accentuated by a flowing white button-down shirt as clean as untouched mountain snow, passing through double doors, radiating with brilliant light on the other side. It was Jesus. He smiled at her with immense love and compassion in His dark brown eyes. It was her Wonderful Counselor; he had been escorting the woman and baby who both died at the clinic that day, home.

Epilogue

For over fifteen years, Lillian had been a runner. It helped keep her anxiety at bay, kept her lean, and helped her outrun many demons. But she was no longer that girl from her youth; she was no longer that woman from just a few months ago. She was a new creation in Jesus Christ. She understood that now, with her intellect and with her heart. She decided to retire her running shoes that weekend in September, after the miracles God performed in her life, and she began to practice yoga instead. After consistent weekly sessions of hot and Vinyasa classes, with pregnancy modifications as her belly grew, her body vibrated with healing blood flow. Surprisingly, the heat of the hot room therapeutically reminded her of the saunas of her youth in Michigan.

The stretching and bending reminded her that she would never break. Deep backbend positions, for as long as she could perform them, reminded her to share her voice and keep her heart open. The peace found while laying on her back in savasana offered mental clarity and the calmness needed for self-reflection, something not easily found in her busy, pulsating world. Rolling over into the fetal position on her right side at the end of every practice reminded her that she was reborn and worthy of love and kindness. It was not because of anything she did, and it did not demand she do anything, but because of what Jesus had already done.

Lillian, who had built a career as a compassionate and professional therapist, a helper of mankind, a guide for many through dark days, found healing and rest from her own demons through the work of God in her and through her own work with her clients. The reckless and relentless love of her husband, coupled with the baby growing inside her, were the cherries on top—the "just because God could" in her life. She'd come to embrace that He wants to bless His people abundantly more than they can fathom.

Her faith restored, and again full of the wonderment of God, she realized she was nothing without Jesus in her. And then, because He was in her, she was everything. She had always been a daughter of the King, and was now a blessed wife, a forgiving daughter, and a worthy mother. It was the Holy Spirit inside her who was sent as a Helper. As a willing seed planter, she would continue to reconcile the darkness of mankind by reminding her clients that there is healing in Jesus. Even if she couldn't talk about Him unless clients brought Him up in sessions, she could show Him to others by her love. It was the greatest of love stories that she would continue to tell every opportunity she had.

Without looking back, except to see how far she had come, and to remember what Jesus had done for her, she moved forward unapologetically, like a warrior on a battlefield. No longer just surviving, she was now making a choice to thrive. Not living to please her enemies or gain their favor, she had learned to pray for them, so their hearts would soften to a greater message.

Knowing the darkness would continue to attack, intensely and purposefully, especially as she grew closer to the light, she held on to the promise that Jesus had already overcome the dark through His death and resurrection. Lillian would do good works, not to gain anything, not because she had to, not to boast, but because she wanted to produce fruit. Fruit was the proof of her promised salvation in Christ, to complete God's purpose for her life. She pressed on, navigating the temporary earth until her Father God chooses to bring her home to His eternal glory.

About the Author

*A*manda Elyse Bleak, born and raised as a Michigander, calls Florida home. She achieved a Bachelor of Arts degree from the University of Miami, majoring in Psychology, and a Master of Science degree from Palm Beach Atlantic University in Counseling Psychology. She currently is a Licensed Mental Health Counselor working passionately to empower children, adolescents, and families in crisis to find hope and healing. Most importantly, she is a confessed sinner, forgiven and redeemed by the sacrifice of Jesus. Married to her best friend of more than 30 years and blessed with three beloved children and three devoted dachshunds, she finds peace and joy in knowing that there will soon be a day with no more fears, pain, or tears. Until that day, she is determined to help humanity recognize and embrace the beauty from their ashes as she remains an ever-loyal seed planter for the One True God.

Mental Health Resources

If you are in a crisis or emergency, please call 911
Seek a medical or mental health professional in your area for immediate help

The National Child Traumatic Stress Network: nctsn.org
National Center for Child Traumatic Stress (NCCTS)
NCCTS- University of California, Los Angeles 1-310-235-2633
NCCTS- Duke University, Durham, NC, 1-919-682-1552
National Suicide Prevention Lifeline: Call 1-800-273 Talk (8255)
National Child Abuse Hotline: 1-800-4AChild (1-800-422-4453)
    or text Crisis Text Line: Text "HOME" to 741741
National Domestic Violence Hotline: 1-800-799-SAFE (7233)
    or text LOVEIS to 22522
RAINN (Rape, Abuse, and Incest National Network) National Sexual
    Assault Hotline 1-800-656-HOPE (4673)
Substance Abuse and Mental Health Services Administration (SAMHSA)
    1-800-662-HELP (4357)

Printed in the USA
CPSIA information can be obtained
at www.ICGtesting.com
LVHW041120131023
760673LV00044B/624